LOST

TO

You

A.L. JACKSON

A.L. Jackson
www.aljacksonauthor.com
Cover Design by RBA Designs
Photo by **Perrywinkle Photography.**
Formatting by Mesquite Business Services

Print ISBN: 978-1-946420-16-9
eBook ISBN: 978-1-983404-50-4

LOST
TO
You

More From A.L. Jackson

One

CHRISTIAN

She sat across from me, this beautiful girl who had to be both the cutest and sexiest thing I'd ever seen. A rich tenor rang in her words, this modest kind of confidence that sucked me in, while her cheeks seemed to continually light with a gentle flush when she said anything that embarrassed her in the slightest way.

A sublime contradiction, self-assured and shy.

How ironic it was *her*.

But really, I shouldn't have been all that surprised. I always knew what I wanted the moment it saw it.

Shifting against the hard wood of the chair, I leaned forward and struggled to pay attention to the words she spoke as I stared, mesmerized by that perfect mouth.

One elbow was propped on the table, her head tilted to the side as she supported it with her fingertips. Sun-streaked waves of dark blonde hair fell down around one side of her heart-shaped face as she thumbed through the thick textbook resting on the table between us.

Concentration edged her brow, her pouty lips pulling into a thin line whenever she became engrossed in something she read.

"Do you think you're up for this?" she asked, sounding overwhelmed.

"Definitely."

No question.

I was up for all kinds of things.

Last night, I'd shared two short emails with her, and we'd arranged to meet at this little café during the time we both had a break in our classes.

Of course, at that time, I had no idea who my American Government study partner would turn out to be. The little description she had given, I'd scribbled on the note that was now crumpled in my front pocket.

Elizabeth Ayers, long, blonde hair.

At the bottom, I'd jotted down her cell phone number.

Yeah, I'd be holding on to that.

A groan of apparent dread slipped through her lips, and the sound almost caused me to release one of my own.

"Are you sure? Because have you looked through this syllabus?"

She glanced up, then back at the small stapled pack of papers laid out between us. "There's going to be a ton of memorization. I'm pretty sure this is going to be a pretty difficult class," she said seriously, completely focused on the information she was devouring as her eyes roved over the page.

"You have no idea how happy I was to find that sign-up sheet for a study partner. I don't know about you, but I can't afford to get a bad grade in this class." She scribbled something in her notebook, licked her lips, rambled mostly to herself.

And I just stared.

Fifteen minutes ago, before I'd walked through the door of the café and seen her, I'd been all wrapped up in this grade, too. I'd been just as worried about who my partner would be. I'd figured it'd be my luck to get paired with some loser who would take advantage of my time and my hard work. I'd have dealt with it, too, sucked it up and worked my ass off because I had no other choice.

There was no way in hell I'd give my dad

another reason to ride me because I had a grade slipping below his approval.

But no, I'd walked through the door and it was *her*.

Since then, I'd had a really hard time focusing on anything but the fluid lilt of her voice and the amber warmth of her soft brown eyes.

Shock had frozen me in the doorway when I walked through the door of the café and was met with the face of the same girl I hadn't been able to shake from my mind since the first day of our American Government class last week.

When the class had been dismissed, I gathered my things and stood to leave. Looking up to make my way down the aisle of steps, I'd glimpsed just the side of her face when she'd cast a furtive glance behind her as she'd been heading out the door.

My breath had caught.

Since then that face had slipped in and out of my mind, creeping into my thoughts, making recurrent appearances in my dreams.

My reaction to her had been just as strong when I walked through the door today.

Girls didn't do this me. And she'd managed it twice. Sitting across from her now, I knew I had to have her.

Even if it was only once.

Pausing, she looked up at me, her eyes narrowed in what appeared both humor and mild agitation.

"Christian, did you hear anything I said?" she asked, her gaze wandering my face for an answer. "Please tell me you're not going to make me do all this work myself."

I attempted to shake off the visceral reaction that had my body itching to take what I instinctively knew would be mine. "Of course, I heard you. Class is going to be a ton of work. I'm good with that." I grinned at her. "And no, I'm not going to make you do all the work."

I nudged her foot under the table with mine, flashing the same smile I'd learned years ago was the surest way to get what I wanted. And what I wanted right then was her. "What kind of guy do you think I am?"

Heat rose to her cheeks. I could almost feel her warmth radiating across my face in confused waves, this sweet shyness that seemed to be lacking from every other girl I'd run across since I came to this city. Lacking in every girl I'd come into contact with in the last four years, really.

I could feel the attraction that mingled with it, though it was flanked by a strong current of self-preservation.

"I haven't figured that out yet," she said as she straightened and pitched her head to the side. She slowly tapped the backside of her pen on her notepad, studying me for intent.

Her steady gaze locked on me, as if she

contemplated who or what I was, while mine was unruly, my eyes wandering on their own accord.

They traveled the curved line of her jaw, down her neck, to the expanse of perfect skin exposed above the V of her T-shirt.

Could anyone blame me that I wanted to bury my face there?

I wondered how long it'd be before she let me.

When I brought my attention back up, her expression had shifted and she sat back, a knowing smirk settling on her face, though it seemed to be hiding something deeper in the warmth of her honey eyes.

It looked a whole lot like disappointment.

An unfamiliar feeling curled in my stomach.

Guilt.

I looked away, down at my hands clenched together on the table in front of me.

Everything about her swam with innocence, but her eyes were too sharp to speak of naivety. She knew exactly what I was thinking as my gaze caressed the soft slope of her neck. Most girls would be crawling all over me by now, but Elizabeth looked like maybe she'd just decided she didn't want anything to do with me.

Swallowing, I tried to reel myself in.

I was fucking this all up, and I had no idea why I cared.

But I did.

I mean, I didn't want a relationship or anything, but I wanted . . . something. The expression on Elizabeth's face told me she'd already decided what that was.

Yeah. Definitely fucking this up. . . .

She went back to flipping through the pages, meticulous as she mapped out our study plan for the semester. She asked me several questions about my strengths, my schedule, when and where I preferred to have our study sessions.

Even though she was so obviously worried about her grade, there was no doubt in my mind she was going to ace this class.

"Where are you from, Elizabeth?" The words were abrupt, and I shifted in my seat, leaning farther across the small table with my elbows digging into the wood, edging her direction.

Honey kissed every inch of her—her hair, her eyes, her skin—and I knew she couldn't be from around here.

"Uh . . . San Diego," she said almost absently, absorbed in the words she wrote, before she surprised me by stopping and looking up at me with a wistful smile. "I lived there my whole life. This is the first time I've been out of California. I still can't believe I'm in New York City. It's crazy."

With a small, contented shake of her head, she bit at her lip and picked up where she'd left off, the fluid sweep of her hand across the paper as she planned.

"This is the first time you've been out of California?" Incredulity dropped from my mouth. How was that even possible?

I'd traveled the world with my parents, forced to go on trip after boring trip. When I was young, I would get excited as I sat in a first-class seat on the plane, antsy to get into the air, to see new things— for my father to be there.

But soon I realized it was always the same.

Me stuck alone in a huge hotel room, playing my old Nintendo Game Boy with a nanny I didn't even know, while my parents went off to do whatever they did.

Vague memories of my mother's promises lingered in my mind, but they were always an excuse, a lame apology that next time she would take me sightseeing or to a theme park or some other cool place I wanted to go.

By the time I was fifteen, whenever they went out of town, I refused to go with them.

"I guess that's not normal for most people," she said, "but my mom raised me and my sisters by herself, so there wasn't a lot of money left for vacations." She lifted her head and I could see her face. A gentle casualness framed her mouth, something that spoke of respect and grace.

My mother would have rather died than admit she lacked the money for something. But here was this girl who couldn't be more than eighteen, laying it all out, setting her private world on display.

And without an agenda.

A tiny laugh slipped through Elizabeth's lips. "But we always had our beach."

For a second, sadness clouded her features, an almost indiscernible twitch of her muscles.

"You miss it," I blurted through a whisper. It wasn't a question. I felt it as it suddenly saturated the air around us.

Shrugging, she began to doodle on the margin of her notepad. "That obvious, huh?" She grimaced a smile. "It just kinda hit me a couple of days ago. I've never been away from home, and here I am, all the way across the country with no friends or family. I mean, don't get me wrong, I worked my entire life to get here, and I'm beyond thankful for it."

She wet her lips, swallowed, and averted her gaze as she hunched her shoulders. "I just really miss my mom."

Something that resembled pain struck me deep in the chest. I was so far out of my element, a million miles from what I knew.

What I knew were girls who wanted the exact thing I wanted.

Ones who climbed in my bed without a second thought.

Our intentions were never dishonest, and that

was where it always ended. I never pretended I would give them any more. And they never pretended they wanted anything more from me, either.

But right then, the only thing I knew was I really wanted to hug this girl.

I didn't even know her, though it didn't take a lot for me to realize I wanted to.

"Hey," I said as I leaned in low to capture her gaze, sliding my palm across the table to rest next to her notebook. My fingers twitched, and I resisted the urge to take her hand that lay an inch away. "You're not alone."

I raised a brow, lightening my tone in hope of lightening her mood. "Just think of all the time you're going to have to spend studying with me."

Her head was still bowed when she laughed and looked up at me from under the hedge of hair that had fallen like a veil to the side of her face, though the sadness that had temporarily hazed her expression was gone.

She smiled, and it was as if I could see everything inside of her.

In that moment, I had this strange sense that I knew her better than I'd ever known anyone, even though I really didn't know her at all.

Elizabeth was strong and driven, incredibly intelligent, but what was most apparent was she was genuinely kind.

She emitted a slight snort and raised her own brow. "I don't know if that's a good thing or not, Christian."

It was all tease and truth, playful words loaded with innuendo that confirmed she'd already made assumptions about me.

"How about you?" she asked. "You're from here?"

"Nah, I'm from Virginia."

"Virginia." She seemed to ponder it as if it were some foreign, exotic place. "So what brought you to New York?"

I laughed low, but it lacked any humor. "I've known I would be going to Columbia since I was a little boy."

There was never any choice. Anything less and all my father's careful grooming, priming me for the future he'd picked out for me, would have all been in vain.

Frowning, she reached out to wrap her slender fingers around her coffee mug and sipped at it as she waited for me to continue.

I answered her as simply as I could. "My dad went here."

"Ah." She nodded as if she understood what I meant, as if she recognized she'd hit a nerve. She looked like she was tempted to ask me more.

I quickly changed the subject. My parents were the last thing I wanted to talk about. "So what about you? Why New York?"

She got that wistful smile again, her eyes soft and her words softer. "It's kind of embarrassing, but have you ever had a place that just became a fairy tale to you?"

I blinked, not really understanding, but wishing I could. I offered a little shrug. "No. Not really."

Definitely not.

She reddened again, dipping her chin in the way she did every time she seemed to get self-conscious. "New York has always been like that for me, from the time I was a little girl. I always thought it had to be the most amazing place in the world. Then when I decided I wanted to be an attorney, I knew it had to be Columbia."

"Wait . . . what? You're pre-law?"

She nodded.

Could she be any more perfect for me?

And where the hell did that thought come from?

"Me too," I said.

She sat up, both of us more excited than we probably needed to be. "Really?"

"Yeah . . . you know, my dad's headed a firm for years. Real estate. I'm going to take over for him when he retires."

"Oh God . . . that's amazing." She was grinning, maybe happy for me. Maybe happy to find out we had more in common than we'd initially thought.

"What are you going into?" I asked.

She was still smiling, her body vibrating in her seat. "I'm not sure yet. Some sort of family law . . . I want to work for the state or a non-profit." Passion poured from her mouth, her heavy exhale thick with emotion. She hugged herself, as if she were imagining herself there, what her future would be like. "Something where I can help kids." Her face glowed. "An advocate of some kind. I don't know."

She shrugged, but clearly not because she didn't care. It didn't have to be perfect. It just had to be right.

I was floored.

I'd never met anyone like her.

I knew what those jobs paid. Obviously, Elizabeth did too. She was after the worst position any attorney could ever have, what my father called scrounge work.

For years, he pounded it into my psyche that it would be required before I made it to the top. He wouldn't even consider allowing me into his firm until I'd spent at least two years scrubbing. I expected it to be the two worst years of my life.

And it appeared to be Elizabeth's ultimate goal.

For my dad, it wasn't about giving back. It was about paying dues. He wanted to see me scrape the bottom of the barrel so I'd understand what he was giving me when he ultimately handed me a job on a silver platter.

"What?" she asked when she noticed my expression. Confusion dimmed the light that had glimmered from her face.

I stared at her for too long, my mouth dry and my palms wet. How badly I wanted to climb inside her, to really understand her, to know what it'd feel like not to be driven by money and greed.

But the last thing I wanted was her to see inside of me.

I shook my head. "Nothing. That's just . . . really cool, Elizabeth."

"Thanks, Christian." A humble smile tugged at the corner of her mouth. She flipped the textbook shut and shoved the syllabus into a folder. "I need to get going. Are we good to meet here on Monday, then? Same time?" she asked.

Monday was five days from now. Something inside me protested. I didn't want to wait that long to see her again.

"What are you doing Friday night?"

"Me? Studying." She emitted a low laugh and shook her head as if anticipating what I would say next.

"How about you go out to dinner with me instead?" I asked her anyway. I smiled that smile again.

"That's not going to happen." Red colored her cheeks, but she seemed to be fighting a smile. She gathered a few loose papers and tapped the bottom edge of the pile on the table to straighten them.

"Why not?"

"Because I'm not the kind of girl you're looking for."

"And how do you know what kind of girl I'm looking for?"

She sat back in her chair, leveling her gaze on me.

I fidgeted under it.

All traces of that shyness were gone and set in its place was a steely determination as she lifted her chin high. "Okay then, Christian, answer me something."

I tilted my head. I was so going to regret agreeing to this, but I couldn't help but bite. "All right."

A smile danced in her brown eyes. "How long have you been in New York?"

I let out the breath I was holding. Okay, that was easy. Relieved, I inched a little closer. "My parents had me moved up here at the beginning of the summer. They said they wanted me to have a chance to get used to my surroundings. I figure they just wanted me out of their hair."

She nodded subtly, her brow cinched together as if she'd been struck with some unknown suspicion.

"Are you happy here?" whispered from her mouth as if she were asking me to reveal my darkest secret.

I blinked, caught off guard by the sudden intensity of her voice. "Anywhere is better than spending another minute in my parents' house." I answered her honestly because I found I didn't know how to lie to the girl sitting across from me.

For a second, her expression softened, and she just nodded as she held my gaze. I was pretty sure I'd never felt more exposed than I did in that single moment.

She cleared her throat and looked away, breaking the connection. When she looked back up, everything had shifted, the same challenge glinting in her eyes. "And how many girls have you slept with since you got here?"

Oh shit. Of course, she had to ask the one question I didn't want to answer, voicing the judgment she'd already cast.

"Uh . . . um . . ." I stumbled, then bit down on my bottom lip, shaking my head as I released a self-conscious laugh.

She crossed her arms over her chest, the smile at the edge of her mouth lifting. "What? You can't count that high, or you don't want to tell me?"

Her tone was light, an easy mirth at my expense.

But I could see it, set there in the perfect lines of her face that I wanted nothing more than to trace with the tips of my fingers. She really cared about my answer. She'd baited me, strung me up, and left me with nowhere to hide.

Red-faced, I scratched the back of my neck, knowing no matter what answer I gave, it'd be the wrong one. If I lied, she'd know, and I knew there was no way she'd be okay with the truth.

"Come on, Elizabeth . . . I just asked if you wanted to go to dinner with me."

"So, you're saying you don't want to sleep with me?"

Frustration tumbled from my mouth in a strained groan. Still, I couldn't lie to her.

Like it wasn't obvious how badly I wanted to take her back to my place and coax that blush from every inch of her body. "That's not what I said."

She leaned down to her backpack that was sitting on the floor and slid her things into it. Her face was lifted to look up at me as she did. "Well, then, Christian, I think it's safe to say I'm not the kind of girl you're looking for."

The sharp peal of her zipper announced her departure.

I really couldn't remember ever being turned down before. I'm sure I had, but it'd made little impact on me, something forgotten as I'd immediately moved on to the next and better thing.

This slammed me.

I could do nothing but stare at Elizabeth as she stood and slung her backpack over her shoulders.

It wasn't a sensation I was familiar with, the bite of rejection, but now it had me pinned to my chair.

Why the hell did this bother me so much?

She reached up and pulled out her hair trapped by her backpack, gripping the bulk of it in a fist that she ran down the length. It spread out in a soft wave over one shoulder as she released it.

I swallowed.

God, looking at this girl and not being able to touch her was complete torture.

"I'll see you around," she said, taking a step toward the door. She twisted to look at me, walking backward as she spoke. "If you don't find anything better to do Friday, I'll be studying. You have my number."

She grinned, and all I could do was laugh. I was definitely not expecting that.

She spun back around, and for the first time, I was able to appreciate her perfect ass in those tight jeans.

No, I definitely didn't have anything better to do on Friday night.

Shit.

I was in so much trouble.

"It's a date," I hurried to call after her.

She swung the door open, shaking her head with a small laugh. "No, Christian, it's not."

two

ELIZABETH

Oh, he was so off limits. So unbelievably off limits.

The door to the café shut behind me with an echo of his throaty laughter tickling my ears.

I hit the sidewalk, hurrying to put some space between us. I had five more minutes I could have stayed before I needed to leave for my next class, but I was getting out of there before he talked me into something I would definitely regret.

People swarmed around me as I cut a path against the flow of the approaching crowd. I muttered unheard apologies toward my feet, edging off to the right and blending in with the bodies heading back toward campus.

I hiked my backpack higher and tried to rid my mind of him.

There was no way I could allow myself to get lost in this guy, and by the thoughts *that* smile had left swirling through my head—that stomach-flipping, heart-lurching, earth-shattering smile—I knew just how easily I could.

Oh God.

Christian Davison had to be the most gorgeous guy I'd ever seen.

The second I noticed him walking through the door, I'd been caught in the darkness concealing his face, the halo of light streaming in behind him partially casting his face in shadows.

It was as if my body knew what hid behind them was worth waiting to discover.

And damn, if it wasn't right.

The door had slipped shut when he inched forward, swallowing the shadows and revealing an unruly shock of the blackest hair I'd ever seen. Pair that with those blue eyes, and I was lost.

They were so intense.

So unsettling.

His jaw was all sharp angles and hopelessly losing the battle with a coat of coarse stubble that was just as dark as the hair on his head.

But his mouth was flirty and soft—full—

something to smooth out the severity of everything else.

It was the first time in my life I'd had the urge to reach out and touch a complete stranger, to run my fingertips over his jaw, maybe across his lips, wondering how his skin would feel under mine— wondering how *I* would feel doing it.

For a moment, he'd searched the room, before recognition had dawned on his face when his eyes landed on me, his stride purposed as he'd walked my direction.

Each step he'd taken had radiated confidence, those lips curving with an arrogance as he approached.

It only took a couple of seconds for me to understand why his presence had seemed to fill up the entire room. Why he'd seemed to stop time when he walked through the door.

The guy was completely full of himself.

It's not like I was all that experienced, but I wasn't stupid, either. I knew exactly what Christian wanted. It had gleamed in his eyes and rippled through his muscles. I wasn't opposed to guys—to having a boyfriend or someone who cared about me.

What I was opposed to was giving myself to someone like him.

The man would own me with one passing touch, and I was certain that's exactly what it would be.

Passing.

The last thing I needed my first year in college was to get my heart broken by a boy who was undoubtedly after one thing. I didn't work this hard to get here to get my heart trampled.

After all the sacrifices I had made I wasn't about to do something so foolish.

Giving up on most activities my friends had reveled in—the parties, the shopping, the fun—in favor of studying and striving to win every scholarship I could earn.

The extra hours my mother had worked to scrape together a few extra dollars, every grant I'd applied for, and every student loan I had to one day pay back.

I'd worked too hard to waste my time here.

A complication like Christian Davison was something I definitely didn't need.

But man, was he pretty.

The really irresponsible side of me thought it'd be worth the risk.

Something reckless and completely unlike me to add to the list of cherished college memories.

A fling with a boy who would so obviously make me forget myself.

One glimpse of his sure hands and strong body left no question that he would make me experience things I'd never experienced before.

A shiver traveled down my spine and pooled somewhere in my stomach.

Shaking myself out of it, I forced that dangerous train of thought aside.

I knew myself better than that. It wouldn't be a cherished memory, but something that would eat at me for years.

I didn't do flings.

I fell in love, and falling in love with someone like Christian was a mistake I couldn't afford.

But if I could somehow put the unknown longing he created in me aside, I realized I *liked* him. I liked the way he seemed to get lost in thought, disappearing somewhere deeper beneath the façade I doubted few people ever penetrated. I could almost feel it, an undercurrent of vulnerability there beneath his perfect exterior.

Maybe that's what he needed, someone to look past that gorgeous face and his arrogant smile. Maybe he needed a friend in this city as much as I did.

We'd see.

The rest of the week passed in a blur. Every time I stepped out my apartment door, I still found myself in awe, amazed by this city. As much time as I'd spent hoping for it—working for it—there was a part of me that never believed I'd make it.

Even though living here was a lifelong dream, it had taken some getting used to. The mass of people at every turn. The buildings that towered on every side.

There were times when I felt closed in, like the sky could crash down on me and I'd have nowhere to run. But for the most part, I loved it and reveled in this city that I had only known in pictures and movies.

When my last class of the week let out on Friday, I wound my way through the crowds toward my apartment. I'm sure I appeared a tourist, my head raised as I soaked up the details of every building and landmark.

My building was a drab block of gray brick, glued between two taller buildings on each side. I jogged up the stairs to the second floor. Turning the key in the lock, the door opened to my small studio apartment.

Well, small didn't really describe it.

A twin bed was pushed lengthwise up against the far wall to the right, and a miniature kitchen lined the opposite wall to my left. Straight back was the only separate room—a bathroom so small I could fit it in my back pocket.

But I loved it.

It was mine, my own space, a reward for what I'd worked so hard to achieve.

Crossing the five steps to the other end of the

room, I sighed in satisfaction and dropped my backpack to the bed, shrugged out of my jeans, and pulled on some black yoga pants.

If I had to spend my Friday night studying, I wanted to be comfortable.

Flopping onto my unmade bed, I dug out the books I needed from my bag.

Afternoon light filtered in through the window, wrapping the room in a cozy glow. I snuggled up and hunkered down. In order to stay in New York, I had to keep all my scholarships, so I couldn't risk letting any of my grades slip.

I dove into my first class, reading through the materials that were due the next class period.

Late afternoon bled into evening, time passing quickly. The room had begun to darken, and I reached over to twist the switch to the small lamp that rested on the floor next to the bed.

The light bulb flickered on.

A dim light seeped up the back wall and illuminated my book. I figured I couldn't put it off any longer, so I changed to my most dreaded subject—math. If there was one subject that would ruin me, math was it. I flipped to the correct chapter.

My mouth moved slowly as I struggled to absorb the instructions and somehow make sense of the numbers.

I looked to the ceiling and groaned.

Completely hopeless.

My phone rang from the front pocket of my backpack. It was a welcomed distraction.

Mom called me almost every evening, and I was anxious to hear her voice, for her to tell me she missed me as much as I missed her.

Unzipping the pocket, I rummaged around to pull the phone free and glanced at the screen.

But no, it wasn't her.

I frowned as I stared at the number lit up on the screen. It was a number I really hadn't anticipated seeing tonight.

Actually, I was kind of shocked.

It didn't mean his face hadn't fluttered in and out of my consciousness over the past week or that I had forgotten that smile. It just meant when I made the offer, I never really believed he'd take me up on it.

A flicker of excitement sparked in my stomach. I chalked it up to being lonely.

Accepting the call, I placed it against my ear.

"Hello?" I realized I was smiling. No doubt, he could blatantly hear it coloring my voice.

Ridiculous.

"Hey, Elizabeth, it's Christian." His voice was easy, filled with the same confidence he'd approached me with at the beginning of the week. This time it didn't throw me. I expected it. Welcomed it, even.

"Hi, Christian. What are you up to?"

"I just got out of my last class for the day. Wanted to find out where you're studying."

"Um . . ." I glanced around my tiny apartment that I could only imagine was smaller than Christian's closet.

I tried to picture him here.

Ridiculous.

"I'm actually studying at my place." I bit at my lip, and I couldn't help but tease, "What, no hot date for the evening?"

His voice dropped low, hinting at humor and something else I didn't want to recognize. "What, you didn't believe me when I said I was going to spend the evening studying with you? You're going to learn to trust me, you know."

I shook my head, trying not to laugh. "Is that so?"

"Yes, that's so." A current of suggestion slipped through his voice. This guy had to be the most dangerous predator walking the streets of New York City.

So why did I seem to like him so much?

I rattled off my address, then told him, "All right then. I'll be waiting."

Ending the call, I hopped off my small bed and ran around to pick up the dirty clothes I'd left in random piles around the room.

It wasn't like the studio was dirty—it was just

cluttered.

My arms were full of clothes when there was a tap at my door.

I tossed them into the hamper next to my bed before rushing over to unlatch it.

And just like he promised to be, Christian, in all his perfect glory, stood at my door.

Oh God.

Men should not be that pretty.

And of course, he had to unleash that smile on me. "Hey, Elizabeth."

Again, with the stomach flip.

He shouldered his way into my apartment before I had time to step out of his way. He huffed out a weighted breath as he turned a slow circle to take in my apartment, a casual smile on his face when he turned back to me. "You don't know how happy I am it's Friday. How about you?" he asked.

"Yeah, I'm ready for a little down time," I admitted, closing the door behind us, stopping to admire him standing in the middle of my room.

He didn't look so out of place, after all.

"I think I'm finally getting a handle on my schedule and routine." I sidestepped around him and crossed the room, moved some papers around to make a place for him to sit down on my bed/couch. "I was pretty overwhelmed last week, but I'm getting used to it. Finding my way around the city isn't as hard as I thought it would be."

I grinned and gestured to the spot I'd cleared. "Make yourself at home. I don't exactly have a lot of space."

He looked around again. "Yeah . . . I kind of noticed that."

Without any hesitation, Christian plopped down on my bed like he belonged there. Shrugging his backpack from his shoulders, he scooted back to rest against the wall, his long body sprawled across the width of the bed with his feet hanging over the edge.

Dull light glinted off the playful blue eyes looking back at me after they made a pass over my bed. "But I think we could make it work."

I rolled my eyes. "Don't you wish."

Christian just laughed.

"And don't go knocking my apartment," I said as I curled back onto my spot on the bed. I grabbed my textbook and pulled it onto my lap. "This place is perfect for me, don't you think?"

He shook his head as if he didn't understand me at all. A mild chuckle rumbled in his chest.

We both knew there was no denying my place was kind of a dump.

He sobered, his words not quite matching the confused expression on his face. "You really like it here?"

It wasn't mocking, just an honest question as he searched my face for the truth.

"You don't work so hard for something and not appreciate it, even if it isn't the nicest place in the world."

His smile was soft. "Well, I guess it's perfect, then, Elizabeth."

His expression shifted into something I couldn't quite grasp, something that worked to unravel all the reservations I held twisted inside of me. The smile slipped from his mouth, his head angled as his gaze seemed to swallow me whole.

I could almost taste him, the heavy breaths he panted filling the air, diminishing the space between us.

He was a walking contradiction, flipping from this joking, easygoing guy who seemed to understand this was a study session, to this extreme intensity that threatened to set my skin on fire.

I wondered if anyone else noticed it. Wondered if they could see what simmered and churned in the blue of his eyes.

Something real and genuine and consuming. Something that left me more unnerved than I'd ever been in my life.

I struggled to curb my reaction to him, fought the part of me that liked it.

Craved it.

The part of me that wished he'd give in and succumb to what I saw so vividly playing out in his eyes.

But that would be a very bad idea.

No way could I allow him to set me off kilter in my own home. I couldn't allow him to detract from the reason I was here or the decision I'd made on Monday.

If Christian wanted to hang out, if he wanted a friend, that was cool. I could handle that.

The truth was, I wanted him here.

But anything beyond a friendship wasn't going to happen.

I just wasn't really sure Christian understood the difference.

When I tore my eyes from his penetrating gaze, he dug into his backpack and pulled out its content. His casual indifference made a reappearance. "So what are we working on tonight?"

I held up my Calculus I book. "Well, I was working on my calculus assignment. Math isn't exactly my strong point."

This time when Christian laughed, it was all throaty and warm, comforting. "Well, you are in luck, Elizabeth, because it's mine. Now if you can help me pass our American Government class, I think we're going to be a pretty good team."

His head tilted as he raised a brow at me. Those blue eyes were both earnest and playful as they traveled my face.

I fought back the blush that crept to my cheeks, the way those words sounded rolling off his tongue, the way he looked at me like I was the most interesting thing in the world.

I was going to have to get used to it if I was going to be around him.

"I think I can handle that," I said.

We settled into an easy rhythm, both of us absorbed in our work. Every once in a while, Christian would lift his head, smile in my direction, as if he needed that small connection.

I'd smile back, welcoming the calm that slipped over my skin.

It was a warmth I knew I could easily get used to.

Yeah, I really liked him here.

With that thought, I closed my calculus book with a loud smack. "Are you hungry? I don't think my brain can process any more numbers tonight."

I hopped off the bed and headed to the kitchen.

"Starving, actually. You ready to take me up on the offer for dinner I made Monday?"

Cocky Christian was back, his movements fluid as he slinked up behind me while I bent down to rummage through the small selection of food I had in the kitchen.

I could feel his presence behind me, larger than it should be, filling up the entire room.

"Um, no." I glanced over my shoulder at him,

unable to hold in the smile. This Christian was just so over the top, but I found he was a whole lot easier for me to handle when he acted this way.

Maybe because it wasn't real. "I think I made that plenty clear then, didn't I?"

"A guy can try, can't he?" He was all tease, moving over to lean back against the one foot of counter space I had in my kitchen with his arms crossed over his chest.

"If he wants to hang out with me, then no, he can't." I nudged him aside.

He laughed, this melodic sound that bounced off my walls and rumbled against my chest.

I filled a saucepan with water and lit the old stovetop with a match. A ring of flames sprang to life. I set the pan over them, pulled out two packets of noodles, ripped them open, and dumped them in. The directions said to let the water boil first, but when it came to food, I was never that patient.

Christian looked horror stricken as he watched the lump of hard noodles soften and separate as the water began to boil. "What are you making?"

"It's ramen. You know, what every poor college student in the country eats?"

Clueless, he shook his head.

Um . . . yeah . . . we were from two very different worlds.

"Are you serious? You've never had ramen

before?" Disbelief colored my tone.

Shaking his head again, he grabbed a fork from the counter. He jabbed at the noodles that roiled in the boiling water as if they were alive, as if he were ready to protect himself if they lashed out to bite him.

"That's disgusting."

"Not disgusting. Delicious. Obviously, you have no idea what you've been missing. Just wait . . . you're in for a treat tonight."

His expression assured me I'd lost my mind. "Whatever you say."

A couple minutes later, I ripped open the foil seasoning packets and mixed them in, and then poured the soup into two bowls.

Shuffling around in the drawer, I dug out two spoons and two forks and dropped them into the bowls.

I handed him one. "You're going to love it."

I turned around, stopping just short of the bed. I slid my back down the wall as I balanced the steaming bowl in my hands.

Settling onto the ground, I stretched my legs out in front of me.

There was no resisting the smile that broke out on my face when I looked up at Christian.

Clearly, standing there, he didn't quite know what to do.

I liked that he could be kind of awkward. That

overbearing confidence stripped away.

"Sit," I said.

He finally gave and moved toward me, settling on the ground beside me and mimicking my position.

His eyes were intent as he watched me twirl some noodles onto my fork, as if he were eager to learn something new.

I tried not to pay attention to how close his face was to mine. How his body felt warn and safe where he sat so close to me.

I blew the lump of pasta before I brought it to my mouth.

From the side, he studied me as is chewed the noodles as if he were learning some secret meaning of life.

Warily, he copied me and tentatively brought a heaping bite to his mouth.

"Oh . . . God . . . that's hot . . . and so good." He went in for a second bite, making these little appreciative noises that expanded my chest.

"See." This time I nudged his foot with mine. "You're going to learn to trust me."

Blue eyes gleamed back at me, his shoulder brushing against mine. "Is that so?"

"That's so." I couldn't help but smirk.

We sat like that on the floor, backs against the wall, our feet stretched out in front of us, eating dinner together.

Comfortable.

Relaxed.

And it felt . . . good.

I realized how thankful I was that he was there. He'd turned what would have been another solitary night into something I was truly enjoying.

Christian released a contented groan and placed his empty bowl on the floor beside him. "Thank you for dinner, Liz."

I rolled my head his direction and murmured, "I'm glad you liked it."

He just nodded, turned back to face forward, and seemed to vanish somewhere inside his head.

Dense silence filled the room.

And I just waited.

Somehow, I knew he needed this. He needed someone who didn't want anything from him. He needed someone who would just listen to him, talk to him, someone who didn't mind sitting beside him without saying a word.

"What's your family like?" Christian barely whispered, breaking through the silence that had taken hold.

His feet rocked back and forth in a slow sway as he tugged at the hem of his shirt.

I could feel the nerves ripple across his skin.

As if he were wondering if he could trust me with the question.

Or maybe he was questioning himself for asking

it in the first place.

He tilted his head to look back at me. He was wearing the same expression that had rocked my foundation earlier.

Genuine and real and open.

It stole my breath.

I didn't know if he'd used his question as a distraction from where ever he had been caught up in his mind or if he really wanted to know about them.

Looking at him now, my gut told me they might be related.

I swallowed, trying to prepare myself to stop into his hidden world, and found my voice. "They're *wonderful*. It's just me, my mom, and my two sisters. My mom . . . she's strong. She taught us to be strong, to work hard for whatever we want in life."

Christian had drifted closer, the side of his thigh pressed against mine. Tonight, his eyes didn't stray from my face, but remained steady, locked on mine, searching.

I fought getting lost in the murky sea that was Christian Davison, in the places he didn't allow people to invade, but seemed willing to show me now.

When he didn't look away, I continued, "My dad left when we were young. It was rough on my mom, but she never let it ruin her. She worked so hard to take care of us. Even though she worked long hours, she always made the time to make each of us feel special. Of course, my sisters and I had to take care of the house and each other while she was at work, but it just made us all closer."

I stuttered through a self-conscious laugh when I felt tears welling up. "We're all really close, have always been."

I quickly wiped the moisture away. "I'm sorry . . . I didn't mean to get all emotional on you. This is the longest I've gone without seeing any of them."

I forced a smile, wondering how this moment had gone from light to heavy in ten seconds flat.

Christian seemed to have that way about him.

"Don't apologize. I wanted to know," he said with a gentle curve of his mouth, and I realized he'd inched away, an almost indiscernible separation, but one I knew had been purposed.

I shook myself off and turned back to look at him in the dimness of the room. "So what's your family like?"

He lifted one shoulder, dropped it just as quick. "You know the story . . . workaholic dad, self-absorbed mom, not much to tell."

"I'm sorry." I resisted the urge to reach out and smooth the pained lines creasing his forehead.

"Don't be." Christian sighed and ran his palms down the length of his thighs, breaking the tension in the air. "I should get going. This was really cool,

Elizabeth. Thank you."

I didn't know if I should admit it, if he would take it wrong or if he would misunderstand, but I decided to tell him anyway. "I'm really glad you were here."

Even if he did take it wrong, think I wanted something I couldn't give him, I wanted him to know it was the truth.

"I love being in New York, but tonight was the first night since I got here that I didn't feel so alone." My smile was soft.

Christian had filled that place in me that needed someone.

A friend.

Someone to listen.

three

CHRISTIAN

From her doorway, Elizabeth watched me walking down her hallway. I kept glancing behind me, making sure she was still there. The way she had her head cocked, her blonde hair fell in sheets of gentle waves over one shoulder, and that same smile that had torn me up the entire night whispered at the edges of her mouth.

All I wanted to do was turn around and bury my hands in those waves.

Tilt her head up and press my lips to hers.

She'd taste sweet.

I'd put money on it.

She'd have to rise to her toes to meet me, and I could almost feel the way the length of her body would mold against mine as she struggled to get closer.

The need was strong, so close to being overpowering.

Shit.

I had to get away from her and put some distance between us.

Right before I rounded the corner, I paused.

Something inside me clenched with the thought of leaving her there. I just stared at her, having no idea how I felt or what I wanted to say.

Knowing I was acting like a freak, I forced myself to say something. "Lock up behind me, okay, Elizabeth?"

Maybe it was lame.

But I just . . . wanted her to be safe.

Needed to know she was safe.

Confusion fluttered across her face. Then she smiled and gave a little wave of her hand. "Of course. Good night, Christian."

I nodded once in her direction and turned the corner.

Elizabeth disappeared behind me, and I couldn't shake the feeling that I was walking away from something that I shouldn't.

Hating the strange feeling, I flew down the stairwell and out into the heavy night air.

Outside, it was still hot, the skin at the nape of my neck beading with sweat that I wasn't positive had anything to do with the humidity hanging in the air.

I just didn't understand this.

I couldn't put a finger on what I was feeling.

I didn't know if I should embrace it or run from it.

On Monday at the café, I couldn't help but think Elizabeth was the most beautiful girl I'd ever seen.

I'd flirted.

Messed with her.

Coaxed the shyness from her because it was just so freaking cute.

I knew I wanted something more than I normally did from a girl. That I wanted to know her and see that smile light her face.

But tonight—tonight was entirely different. Tonight, she had made me feel *different.*

I mean, yeah, I wanted her.

Badly.

I'd had a really hard time keeping the images at bay, ones of wrapping my hands around her thighs and tugging her away from the wall. I could almost hear her book hitting the floor when I shoved it aside and pressed her body into the bed with mine.

It's what came naturally, what I would normally do, the instinct I had to reach out and take what I wanted.

The thing was, she'd made it abundantly clear we weren't crossing that line.

That didn't mean I missed the way she reacted to me. The way she'd flush and shift beneath the attraction that made her uncomfortable.

Part of her wanted me, too.

But there was something that hung in that room that held me back. Something in the softness of her eyes and the in sweetness of her voice.

Elizabeth had to be the most transparent *good* girl I'd ever met.

I couldn't—wouldn't—take advantage of that. It made me sick to think of tainting her.

Knowing me, I'd take what I wanted, get bored, and push her aside. I wouldn't mean to, but I'd hurt her, and I couldn't stand the thought of doing something so vile.

She asked me to be her friend, and I wasn't going to fuck that up by giving into the overwhelming urge I had to touch her.

I could deal with it.

Elizabeth could see through all my bullshit, anyway.

A sarcastic huff escaped my mouth.

I think I was sorely underestimating Elizabeth.

The girl could probably see straight into my soul.

Chances were, she wouldn't let me touch her if I

tried.

With a mumbled groan, I rubbed the tension from my face and dug my cell from my front pocket. Tom was on speed dial, and he answered on the second ring after I'd dialed.

"Hey, man, what's up?" Tom yelled over the deafening background noise. Music thrummed above the roar of indistinct voices. It sounded like the perfect escape.

"Just wondering what's happening tonight."

"We're all at Sam's. You headin' over?"

"Count me in. I'll be there in twenty."

At my building, I took the stairs two at a time and let myself into my apartment.

Dropping my backpack to the floor, I shed my button-up for a fitted black tee and headed into the bathroom where I wet my hands under warm water, splashed some on my face, and ran two hands through my hair to tame the mess it'd become.

I straightened and caught a glimpse of myself in the mirror. A grin clung to my face, something I doubted I could dispel if I tried. I realized I felt good.

Really good.

Tonight had been . . . fun.

Refreshing.

Grabbing my keys, I headed out the door and jogged the two blocks to Sam's place. I could hear the music pulsing as soon as I landed on his floor.

With a single knock against the door, I let myself in.

Bodies were cramped nearly wall to wall.

It definitely wasn't the smallest apartment I'd been in since I'd gotten to New York, especially considering I'd just left Elizabeth's.

I still couldn't make sense of the way she'd looked at the place as if it were a palace.

But here, it felt suffocating. People were packed into the tight space.

Some were huddled in groups where they conversed along the walls. Others pressed and throbbed against each other as they moved in rhythm to the music on the makeshift dance floor in the middle of the room. More were piled on the two couches or sat on the floor.

"You made it!" Tom yelled. He had a red cup lifted over his head as he shouldered through the crowd and cut a path to meet me. He pushed out a fist for me to bump.

I returned it.

"Hey, Tom, how's it going?"

"Great, man, great. Look at this place."

I met him when I first got into town. He was from here, had some connections and knew the area. He was cool, a decent guy, my passport to Friday night.

He was the one who always knew where it was

happening and where I wanted to be.

Sam's was often it.

"I see what you mean," I told him, letting my gaze move along a ton of girls wearing next to nothing.

"I knew you would," he said, setting a hand on my shoulder and beginning to lead me back through the crowd.

"Christian, good to see you finally showed up." Jon gestured with his chin, clapped me on the back as I passed. "Where have you been all night?"

I lifted both hands with a shrug, could feel the smirk splitting my face. "Studying."

"Ah . . . sure you were." He laughed and went back to his beer and the girl hanging on his arm.

There were quite a few people I recognized.

These kind of Friday nights had become my regular.

The same faces.

The same welcome.

I shook hands with a couple guys and hugged a few girls.

Tom continued to shout in my ear about who was where and what had been happening, the girls who'd asked for me.

Asshole made a good wingman, that was for sure.

"Christian, my man." Sam smiled as I approached. He slung his arm around my shoulders and maneuvered us around a group of people I'd never seen before.

At the kitchen entrance, he stopped and waved inside. "There's a keg and lots of ladies. Make yourself at home."

"Sure thing."

I always did.

I grabbed a red cup, filled it until foam overflowed at the sides, and downed it in one breath.

The beer was a little too warm as it glided down my throat, but it wasn't enough to keep me from refilling my cup.

I chatted with a couple people in the kitchen, drank a couple more beers, and refilled my cup again before I wove back out into the main room.

Music pumped through the room.

It amplified the slight buzz I felt coming on.

I sat down onto the floor with my back propped up on the couch, my knees drawn up with my feet flat on the ground and breathed out a sigh of relief.

One night a week, I allowed myself to forget it all.

All the pressures my parents piled on me.

The push to be the best.

The drive to always work harder.

For these few hours, I didn't allow the words my father had drilled into my brain my entire life affect me.

I just . . . forgot.

Joked around with a few of the guys I'd kind of gotten to know. And if I hooked up with some girl?

Yeah, I wasn't going to complain about that, either.

I snorted at myself.

Really, that was the goal. Hang out with the guys and then go home with someone.

One single intention.

Just feeling good for a few hours.

Sam and Tom stood on the other side of the coffee table, provoking each other, little jabs and shoves, the two so blitzed out neither could stand up straight.

I knew what was coming.

The two couldn't seem to keep from making fools of themselves. I was always glad I remained on this side of the show, there to make fun of them for the stupid things they did.

I wondered how many brain cells I lost every weekend just being in their presence.

The sad thing was, I actually enjoyed it. Especially when I'd gotten a few beers in my system, and I was feeling as loose as I was right then.

A slight numbness weighted my arms and legs, and a dull thrum hummed in my ears.

"I think shots are in order," Sam announced. He

disappeared into the kitchen and emerged a minute later with a bottle of tequila and plastic shot glasses.

"Who's up for a friendly wager? Last one standing gets the pot," Sam said, offering up a challenge.

Every weekend, it was the same.

Tom and a couple other guys each tossed down twenties. As always, I passed, though I partook in the pouring and slammed three shots myself.

The room spun a little, and I scrubbed both palms over my face and tried to focus. There was movement at my side, and I looked to the spot where the toe of a heeled boot tapped my thigh.

My gaze traveled up the long body.

Lisa stood there, her full lips pulled into a flirty smile, her tanned legs exposed below the mini skirt she wore. "Mind if I join you?"

I grinned.

This. This was what I needed. Something to undo the knot Elizabeth had tied so tight inside me. The alcohol barely disguised it, distorted an ache I didn't entirely understand.

All I knew was I had to satisfy it.

I inched over to make Lisa room. "Not at all."

I'd hung out with her before, had actually had real conversations with her a time or two. She was nice enough, maybe a little out of place here, like she was testing herself, learning who she wanted to be.

She'd been the one who'd come after me the first time, not that I minded. She seemed pretty laid back, easy in every sense of the word. We got along just fine.

My blurred gaze fixated on her thighs as she awkwardly climbed down to settle beside me. She twisted her torso, just enough that when I looked her direction, we were face to face, nose to nose. I realized how hot I was right then, how my skin tingled and need coiled in the pit of my stomach.

Fingers traveled up my shirt, fluttered across my chin, her mouth a breath from mine. "I was hoping you'd be here."

"You were, huh?" Cocking my head, I looked into the brown eyes staring back at me. They were completely the wrong kind of brown, dark chocolate and rimmed in black.

Not light and tinged with honey. Not knowing and kind.

I blinked the thought away.

"I was hoping you would be here, too," I mumbled at the side of her face, my nose brushing the length of her jaw.

Of course, she hadn't really crossed my mind since the last time I left her apartment more than four weeks ago.

She ran her fingers through my hair, kissed across my face, and murmured at my ear, "I missed—"

I didn't give her time to finish. I just covered her mouth with mine to cut off whatever words she was going to say that would ruin the understanding we had. I kissed her for what felt like forever, my senses filled with the sting of heavy perfume and a thickness that had my pulse beating erratically.

I fought whatever I was feeling.

It was this ridiculous sensation that urged me to push her away.

Ignoring it, I kissed her deeper, swept my tongue against hers, and dipped my hands into her brown hair.

With a short gasp, she broke the kiss. "Wanna go back to my place?" she asked with her body pressed up against mine. Loud music pulsed against our skin, driving the need higher inside of me, something foreign and unpleasant.

"Yeah, let's get out of here."

That's all I wanted, to get out of there, to remove myself from what was gnawing under the surface of my skin.

I climbed to my feet and stretched my hand out to help her stand. With her hand in mine, I dragged her through the mass.

Tom stood near the door, talking too loud and too close to some poor girl's face. He glanced up as I approached, a knowing smirk overtaking his mouth. "See you next weekend, man."

I didn't reply, just raised my hand over my head to announce my goodbye and got Lisa out of there as fast as humanly possible.

The second we were in the hall, her mouth was on my chin and moving over my jaw. Her hand smoothed its way over my chest, up my neck, and into my hair.

My hands dove back into her hair, and I was kissing her and stumbling back as we made our way down the hall.

Seconds later, she had me in the elevator. The low bleep of the button indicated we'd made it to the seventh floor. I backed down her hall, my hands on her hips as I edged us toward her apartment. My back hit her door with a thud.

"Christian," she mumbled.

I was pinned against the wood.

It burned into my skin, hard and cold.

I realized right then that I was sensing too much, the numbness I craved every weekend absent, my hands and mind frantic as I tore at Lisa to get her closer.

But it was Elizabeth's face in my head. Her soft skin under my hands. My fingers digging into her hips.

I jerked my face back from Lisa, raised it to the ceiling, and sucked in a breath as I forced the image aside.

Lisa's mouth went to my exposed neck as she blindly fumbled through her purse. Metal clinked as she withdrew her keys. She reached around me to wiggle one into the lock and let us into her dark apartment.

I already knew the way to her room. I had been there several times.

I palmed Lisa's slender hips and flattened my body against hers. And Elizabeth was still there, her hips curvier, her round ass fitting perfectly in my hands.

I groaned, and Lisa giggled.

Fuck.

My hands snaked under her shirt, my palms gliding up her sides as I pushed it over her head.

Oh God.

My mouth came down aggressively against Lisa's as I palmed her breast in my hand, anything to fill up and shut out whatever was resisting this from happening tonight.

Lisa ripped my shirt over my head, went for the buttons on my jeans while I kicked off my shoes. Her skirt was on the floor, and I was pushing her to her bed.

I climbed between her legs.

The only thing I saw was Elizabeth. Could do nothing but imagine what she'd look like lying there, instead.

How soft she would feel.

How *this* would feel different.

I could never have Elizabeth, but still, I knew I couldn't do this. I couldn't fuck some girl while I pictured Elizabeth's face. It was wrong—disrespectful to Lisa—but what I really cared about was the overwhelming feeling that it was even more disrespectful to Elizabeth.

Unwelcomed hands were at my waistband, pushing down my underwear. I struggled back, got to my knees, and pinned her arms at her sides.

For a moment, confusion filled Lisa's eyes, before a slow, sexy grin took her over, misunderstanding seeded in the manipulated compliance.

I dropped my head, and a heavy, regretful breath forced from my lungs. "I can't do this, Lisa."

The confusion was back, a mix of hurt and anger and embarrassment.

"What did I do? I don't understand."

I released her arms, and she reached for me, her fingertips just grazing across my bare chest as her eyes and mouth implored, "Please."

I understood it then.

Saw it.

All the times I'd done this, and then walked out the door, left some girl alone after I'd used her up, many times when I didn't even know her name.

Was I really blind enough to believe that they

were just like me, that one night was all they ever wanted, and that they never gave me a second thought once I was gone?

Because when I looked down at the blow I'd just inflicted on Lisa, I knew that was not the case. She'd thought of me, wanted me.

"I'm sorry, Lisa." Scooting off her bed, I fumbled to get back into my jeans. I grabbed my shirt from the floor and tugged it over my head. "I can't do this anymore."

She looked away, to the wall, and covered her breasts with the drape of her arm. "You're an asshole."

The statement came so quiet, yet its truth consumed the room.

"I know." I guess it was something I'd always known. It was just the first time I'd admitted it.

I left her there, took the stairs because I needed to burn off some of this unspent energy.

Elizabeth had gotten under my skin. Exposed who I really was just by reflecting her light onto me.

She didn't have to voice it. It was spoken in the way she resisted me the first day, in the assumptions she made that weren't really assumptions at all because they were nothing but the truth. It was clear in the way her eyes clouded with a token of distrust, a barrier she had to place between us to protect herself from me.

Because Elizabeth knew she could just as easily be like Lisa, left alone upstairs, instead of my friend who I couldn't wait to see again.

I ran back to my apartment and let myself into the darkness. I went straight into the bathroom and blasted the showerhead, turning it as hot as it would go.

I shucked my clothes.

Steam filled the room, and I stepped into the water and welcomed its relief. Hot sheets blanketed my back, and I raised my head, let the waves flow down my face, let it wash the night from my body.

Stepping from the shower, I toweled myself off, slipped into a pair of boxers, and fell back against my bed.

I lay, staring at the ceiling, not knowing what the hell I was supposed to do. I was completely mixed up, but in some strange way, I felt okay with it.

Shaking my head at myself, I grabbed my phone. It was just before one in the morning. Earlier than I normally would come crawling back to my apartment, but late enough that Elizabeth would probably think I was complete freak if I gave in and called her just to check that she'd had a good night.

Instead, I tapped out a message and pushed send.

I was shocked when my phone buzzed a few

seconds later. I couldn't help but smile when I read the words.

Elizabeth: Sleep well, Christian.

ELIZABETH

A tiny sigh escaped my lips as I clutched my phone to my chest. Darkness crawled along my ceiling, all except for a thin strip of light that slanted off to one side as it snuck through the top edge of the blind.

It turned out I was right about Christian.

There was no doubt the first impressions were true, too, the ones about the girls and how quickly he flew through them. I knew if I wasn't careful, I could so easily end up one of them.

But beyond that, he was kind.

And he needed a friend.

I reread the text I received a few minutes earlier.

Christian: Wanted to tell you how much tonight meant to me. TY Elizabeth.

It was late, though the city was still alive, horns and sirens echoing outside my door, magnifying how intensely quiet it was within the walls of my apartment.

And I felt warm. Good. Thankful.

Thankful Christian had become a part of my life.

four

CHRISTIAN

The next Friday, Elizabeth and I were back at the café where we first met. Even though we'd just met here yesterday, we decided to meet again tonight so we could cram in a few extra hours of studying for our first American Government quiz next week.

Elizabeth downed the last of her coffee. "So, I think I've finally got it," she said, though her tone hinted that she was only trying to convince herself, her head nodding as if she were mentally calculating another problem.

Of course, I'd spent most of the time trying to

help her with her calculus homework, trying to ingrain these concepts that continued to try to slip right over the top of her head.

Finally, it seemed to have snapped into place, this light flicking on and warming the honey of her eyes. I'd just sat there, staring as she came to understanding, wondering why I felt like some inflated hero when she looked at me like that.

Now she chatted ceaselessly, as if I'd managed to toss the weight from her shoulders. "I really didn't think I would. I mean, I studied it again and again and it just wouldn't sink in."

She climbed to her feet and grabbed her backpack from the floor. She flopped it on the table and began stuffing her things inside. There was nothing ditsy in her words, just this thankfulness that oozed from her mouth. "Thank God I met you, Christian."

She glanced up at me with a gentle smile.

I was so right on about her. She was the nicest girl, innocent and sweet.

And sexy as all hell.

That was the only problem with this whole friendship thing. How could I reconcile the respect I had for her and want to peel the clothes from her body every single time I saw her?

I was pretty sure something in that equation didn't add up.

I smirked at her just because I liked the way she

blushed every time I did. "Now you owe me."

She blushed deeper at the insinuation and dropped her head, and I couldn't help but wonder just how innocent she was. I knew I had to watch myself, to keep everything that wanted to push its way out in check if I was going to successfully walk this fine line.

I gathered my things. "You ready?"

She looked up as the redness from her face slowly seeped away. "Yeah, let's get out of here."

We turned and headed in the direction of her apartment.

She glanced at me, smiling. "So, are you walking me home?"

"It's on my way."

She laughed because we both knew it really wasn't, though it wasn't completely out of the way, either. Just in the wrong direction by two short blocks.

No big deal.

We wandered casually through the evening crowd, neither of us in a hurry, just satisfied to be in the other's company. I liked that it could be so easy with her.

Elizabeth continued to talk as we approached her building, while my attention darted to the guy leaning against her wall as we passed.

Elizabeth didn't seem to even notice him, her consideration fully on me as she ambled toward her door. But there was just something that didn't sit right.

He tilted his chin up, enough for his eyes to take her in.

This instinctual protectiveness rose up from somewhere inside me, an urge to wrap my arm around her waist and pull her to my side.

Of course, Elizabeth had to live in the shittiest building she possibly could, and on top of it, lived by herself.

I hated it.

She paused at her door, rocked back on her heels, and hooked her thumbs in her backpack straps. "So maybe I'll see you around this weekend?"

My eyes went back to the guy against the wall. There were plenty of freaks in New York City. Most seemed harmless and didn't garner a second thought.

Not this guy.

There was just something about him that nagged at my consciousness.

I looked back at Elizabeth. Not a chance in hell would I leave her here by herself.

I shrugged nonchalantly. "I don't have any plans tonight. Why don't we order in and watch a movie, or something?"

Her eyes narrowed in speculation, as if she was thrown off by my sudden suggestion.

I looked back at the guy who was obviously watching us. I guessed I was thrown, too.

"Two Fridays in a row?" She peeked back at me with her brow raised high, then pulled the door opened and held it wide for me as she passed, already expecting me to follow. "Are you sure you're not trying to get into my panties?"

I choked out a laugh as I followed her in.

Did she have any idea how that sounded coming from her mouth? I shook my head and jogged up the stairs behind her.

Apparently, Elizabeth was missing a really important distinction. I wasn't trying to get into her panties. I was trying desperately not to.

She let us into her apartment. It was messier than last week, a week's worth of clothes strewn around on the floor.

"Sorry. Let me pick up really quick. I wasn't expecting company."

She dashed around the small room, plucking up shirts and underwear and random mismatched socks. She balled them up in a pile her arms before she heaved out a satisfied breath as she tossed them into the hamper against the wall. "All done."

God. Did she really have to be so fucking adorable?

"So"—she swung her hands out to clap them in front of her—"are you hungry?"

"I could eat."

She brushed past me as she wandered into the kitchen area. She opened a drawer where she'd stuffed a bunch of menus. "What are you in the mood for?"

I wandered over and sat on the edge of her bed. "Chinese?"

"Sounds good to me," she agreed. Pulling her phone from her back pocket, she read over a menu as she walked across the room, then dropped down beside me without thought. "I think this is the best place."

I gestured with my chin toward the menu. "Whatever works for me."

Her face was all knit up in concentration as she studied, mumbled, "So what do you like?"

"Anything beef."

She laughed and drew out a quiet, "*Okay.*"

We settled on Mongolian beef, sesame chicken, and eggrolls. We chatted until the door rang, and I jumped up to pay.

She tried to stop me, but I insisted. "Am I not allowed to buy dinner for my friend?"

Finally, she conceded and grabbed a couple plates from the kitchen. We kicked off our shoes and sat cross-legged on her bed, using the middle as a table. We opened the containers and filled them as we talked.

Again, we hit this rhythm. A tempo I'd never found with anyone else. One where I didn't have to pretend I was someone I didn't want to be. One where she wasn't shy, and her genuine smile lit up the shadowy room.

Elizabeth gave me all the little details of the city she'd grown up in, her favorite places, and the many ways it was different from here. I could feel her love for San Diego in the pitch of her voice. More obvious was her love for the people there.

"Yeah, the water's always a little cold, but you get used to it," she said as she took another bite.

I inclined my head so I could study her, watch her face as it lifted and fell, twisted in animation as she spoke.

"I can't believe in all the places you've traveled, you've never been to San Diego," she said.

"I've been to L.A. a bunch of times, but for some reason, San Diego was never on the agenda." I shrugged and dipped an eggroll into sweet and sour sauce.

Her eyes narrowed in thought. "You should go sometime. I think you'd like it there."

"Yeah . . . I think I'd like that."

She smiled.

So beautiful. I was still trying to adjust to the decision I'd made, this commitment to our friendship and swearing off girls at the same time. I knew they didn't quite match, and if I tried to explain it to someone, they would think I was completely insane.

But somewhere deep inside of me, it made sense. I figured that was the only thing that mattered.

"Do you think you're going to move back there once you finish school? Is that where you want to practice?" I asked.

Elizabeth kind of frowned, as if the suggestion of not returning was completely absurd.

"Definitely." She took a bite of chicken before she continued, "I mean, you know I love it here, and getting to move to New York has been the best experience of my life, but I can't imagine not going back home. My family is too important to me."

"What happens if some guy comes along and sweeps you off your feet, and for some reason, he can't move to San Diego?"

So maybe I wanted to play Devil's advocate.

Her lips pressed together, and a narrow line dented between her brows. She paused like she were truly contemplating my question. "Then I guess somehow that guy would have to become just as important to me as my family. Maybe more important. I guess that's what marriage is all about . . . sacrifice . . . giving up what you want for the other person."

Her eyes were sincere as she looked across at me.

I was stunned. "You'd really give up what you

wanted for some guy?"

This time, she didn't have to contemplate. Instead, her frown deepened, and she turned the question on me. "Wouldn't you? If you really loved someone?"

"I think marriage is more about compromise. Meeting in the middle. Being compatible."

She scoffed a little, kind of shook her head as she soaked up the last of her sweet and sour sauce with her eggroll. "I guess you could look at it that way."

I laughed. "Look at us, playing philosophers. I don't think anyone has it figured out."

Her face softened. "Yeah, I think you're probably right."

Elizabeth tossed her napkin to her plate. "That was really good. Are you finished?"

I nodded. "Yeah," then mumbled, "Thanks," when she grabbed my plate.

"Thank you for dinner," she countered with a grin as she got to her feet.

While Elizabeth rinsed our plates in the sink, I stuffed the empty containers and garbage in the plastic bag left discarded on the floor and tied the handles in a knot so it wouldn't spill.

Stuffed, I lay back with my feet flat on Elizabeth's floor. A minute later, Elizabeth crawled to her bed, her sweet face passing above mine as she climbed up to lean against the wall. She drew her knees up to her chest.

Releasing my satisfaction in a sigh, I patted my stomach, feeling relaxed after the long week of classes and studying.

It was cool it was this way between us, without expectations, just quiet and ease.

I glanced up to the left and caught Elizabeth staring down at me. Red flooded her cheeks, and she dropped her chin.

Or maybe there were all kinds of expectations and Elizabeth was just fighting them, too.

I turned away because I didn't want her to be uncomfortable with me there. "What do you think of New York now that you've been here for a while? Living up to all those childhood fantasies?" I asked toward her ceiling.

"Sure . . . more stressful than I thought, but fantasies are always that way, aren't they? A little disappointing?"

"I suppose."

"I just can't wait for winter." Excitement surfaced in her voice.

"Why?"

She released this little surprised sound, as if I should have already known exactly what she was talking about. "Christian . . . the tree and ice skating at Rockefeller Center."

If it wasn't so out of character for her, I would have sworn she'd added a little *duh* at the end.

I squinted up behind me, looking at her upside down. "Ice skating? Are you joking, Elizabeth? You come all the way to New York City, and the one thing you're excited to do is go ice skating? You have to be the biggest nerd I've ever met," I teased.

Her face puckered in offense, before her mouth dropped open with it. It was cute. Really cute.

"*Nerd*," I mouthed, unable to stop myself from provoking her more.

Her mouth dropped open farther, and I struggled to keep from laughing, but I couldn't hold it in when Elizabeth suddenly lunged at me, her little fingers coming out to jab me in the sides.

"Nerd, huh? Well you"—she did her best to tickle me, to dig her fingers in, while I did my best at shielding myself—"are . . . a . . . jerk."

I crossed my arms over my chest, splayed my hands out to try to deflect her assault. Her hair fell all around my face, the weight of her tiny body pressed over mine.

We were both convulsing with laughter and exertion.

Her eyes were all soft and playful, and I was thinking how damned good it'd feel to kiss her right now.

Would one kiss really make that much a difference? Change this dynamic? Steal her from me?

As if those questions had just played across my face, Elizabeth jerked away, tucking her hair back behind both ears as she straightened herself.

I kind of smiled at her as she slinked back. Then in a flash, she snuck up and slapped me on the stomach. "Jerk."

"Ow!" I clutched my stomach, searching for air since she'd knocked it from me, laughed some more. "Not cool, Elizabeth. That was a cheap shot."

"You deserved it," she said, laughing as she scooted up the bed, grabbing the remote to flip on the television

I sat up on the edge of the bed, turned around, and plucked the remote from her hand. She had one coming.

"Hey." She grappled for it, and I just shook my head.

"Don't even think about it. This is mine." Smug, I turned back toward the television, leaned with my elbows on my knees and began flipping through the stations.

"Just for that, you're going ice skating with me," she mumbled, almost so low I couldn't hear her.

But I did.

"Not a chance, Elizabeth."

She toed me in the rib, this playful thing that took my breath away.

I finally picked out a movie, some comedy I'd

watched what seemed a thousand times in high school.

Elizabeth raised a brow at my selection.

"Just watch it . . . you'll think it's funny. Trust me."

"Where have I heard that before?"

I chuckled, stood up, and stretched. "Mind if I use your restroom?"

"Go ahead."

I took a piss, washed my hands, and scrubbed my palms over my face. Really, I should call it, get the hell out of there. Because I was almost too satisfied spending my Friday night there. Especially since I was supposed to meet up with Tom right about then.

He'd have to get over it.

I flipped off the bathroom light as I stepped back into the main room. The only light came from the frames on the TV. Colors flickered over Elizabeth's face. I climbed to one knee on the bed, stretched so I could peer out the window.

Elizabeth looked up, frowning. "What are you doing?"

My gaze swept the sidewalk. Creepy lurker guy was gone.

"Nothing." I shook my head, settling back to the bed. I could leave and know Elizabeth would be safe.

Truth was, I didn't want to.

"Is everything okay?" she asked.

"Yeah, everything's fine."

Her face kind of crinkled, like she really didn't understand what was going through my head. I guess I didn't really, either.

We turned back to the television, and I sat through the movie I could quote verbatim and just listened to Elizabeth laugh.

At first, she tried to contain it, to cover up her reaction, before she let loose. She laughed so hard she rolled to her side, so hard she was wiping her eyes.

Her little bare feet were situated close to my side. I reached out, my fingertips brushing over her ankle. I looked up at her. "I'm really glad I met you, Elizabeth."

Her eyes smiled. "I'm really glad I met you, too."

***

Faint light filtered into the room. I blinked, orienting myself to my surroundings. A surprised breath escaped my mouth when I realized my nose was pressed to Elizabeth's belly, her stomach rising and falling in her sleep.

I didn't know when I'd fallen asleep, but at some point, she must have gotten up to flip off the television. Now she slept on her side, our bodies curled in an extended S, her head at the top of the bed and my feet hanging off the end.

I lifted myself to my elbow, pitched my head to the side to pop my stiff neck.

My eyes traveled the length of Elizabeth's body. Her shirt had edged up in her sleep, her jeans stretched over her perfect ass.

Black lace and satin pink bows peeked out at me just over the top.

Damn.

I really did want in those panties.

Sighing, I forced myself to climb from her bed and maneuvered her around to cover her with a blanket.

Elizabeth moaned from the depths of sleep and flopped to the other side.

I reached out and brushed her hair back, ran the back of my hand down her face.

Friends.

I nodded as the word clattered through my brain. Then I peeked once more out her window to the vacant sidewalk below.

Maybe I'd overreacted. But could it ever be counted an overreaction when the safety of someone you cared about was at stake?

I glanced back down at her as she slept. *No.* That was impossible.

I couldn't imagine something happening to her. Someone *hurting* her. The thought of it made me sick.

Shit.

Raking my hands through my hair, I released a breath into the quiet of her apartment, gathered my things, and slipped out her door. On the other side, I paused, my hand on the knob. Finally, I jiggled it to make sure it was locked and forced myself down the hall.

five

Christian reached across the table and nabbed a fry from my plate. He'd already devoured his entire meal in what seemed less than two minutes.

I tried to smack his hand as he crammed the entire thing into his mouth. "Hey, didn't your mom teach you any manners?"

He snorted. "Oh, she taught me all kinds of manners. And it's not like you're going to eat them."

I shook my head, unable to grasp how one person could eat so much food. "Seriously, Christian . . . that can't be healthy."

"I'm a growing boy."

I laughed. I really hoped not.

The guy was already too much, this force of energy that still stole my breath when he entered the room.

Over the last four weeks, we'd been hanging out a lot. The friendship we both needed was blossoming, growing, emerging into something indefinable.

I valued it more than I ever believed I could, though remained reserved, fortified behind the barriers I knew instinctively to put into place.

It was an intuitive command to guard my heart and guard it well.

Enforcing that rule had somehow begun to feel hypocritical, a deceitful mask that I hid behind because the thoughts swirling through my head about Christian could not be contained by the definition I'd set for us.

I'd come to depend on his company, thirsted for it, wanted it.

Wanted him.

Days were spent doing my best to ignore the stirring that gripped me inside when I saw him, to ignore how much I wanted to glide my hands over the strength rippling beneath the denim and cloth covering his body.

It was so screwed up, the direction my thoughts veered whenever the man was near, and he was never far because I couldn't get him out of my head.

Here I'd told him nothing could ever happen between us, while I allowed my mind to go there, to imagine what his back would feel like under my fingers as I clung to him, what my bare skin would feel like against his.

I'd never desired before.

I'd been curious but less than enraptured by the idea of sex, then was left wholeheartedly disillusioned by it in the wake of the pathetic experience I'd had.

Until I met Christian.

Now it throbbed in my consciousness and skimmed along my skin.

I wanted to *feel* him.

But I sensed it deep.

He would break my heart.

Just sitting here, I understood somehow that he already was.

Slowly, surely, these little fault lines in my defenses were splintering.

Fissuring.

From across the table, I studied Christian, wondering how one person could shift something so dramatically inside of me, scare me and give me this joy I didn't know what to do with at the same time. How did he make me feel the most insecure I'd ever felt in my entire life, yet manage to make me feel the safest in his presence?

"So, how's your math class going?" Christian wiped a napkin over his mouth, sat back in his chair with a satisfied sigh as he pushed his plate away. Completely casual, he appeared to be unaware of the chaos he created in me.

"Okay, thanks to you."

A smirk pulled at his mouth. "What would you do without me, Elizabeth?"

"Oh, I don't know, find another cute boy to help me with math," I said, anticipating his reaction if I teased him a little.

For a flash, his eyes narrowed. Then a dangerous grin spread across his face. "I'm just dispensable, huh? Easily replaced?" He hunched and lowered, pressed his chest into the table to meet me at eye level, this slow playfulness coming across him. "How about I let you fail next time?"

"Well, how about I feed you the wrong answers when we study for our next government test?" I countered.

He faked a disbelieving laugh, a gentle ribbing that twisted its way straight to my heart. He was so cute like this, like a harmless boy and not the man who made me fearful, not the one who urged me to hold on to my affections, careful not to let them go.

"You're going to feed me the wrong answers, huh? You?" he challenged.

The entire meal, I'd felt his leg stretched under the table, reaching, giving in to casual brushes, then receding as if they hadn't happened.

Now, Christian abruptly extended his leg, wove it between my legs, direct and bold.

My breath caught.

It was the closest we'd ever come to an embrace.

I averted my gaze but couldn't for long because I could feel him staring at me.

His voice dropped. "You, sweet Elizabeth, the most innocent girl I know, are going to feed me the wrong answers? I bet you've never even told a lie."

Heat flooded my face.

He was taunting me, prodding.

Is that what he really thought of me? Innocent?

But honestly, I guessed I was.

Well, maybe not innocent. Just inexperienced.

I had no idea how to play Christian's games, no idea of what the girls he surrounded himself with were like, although I could only imagine. It had to be my greatest disadvantage. Vulnerability oozed from my consciousness, and I shifted in discomfort.

Christian could devour me whole.

His expression shifted as he edged even closer, his voice a whisper, "Just how innocent are you, Elizabeth?"

It was clear what he was asking, though I couldn't tell what he hoped the answer to be. Those blue eyes flamed as he waited, his leg burning against the inside of my calf, the air in the restaurant thick.

I slowly shook my head.

"Not that innocent, Christian," I whispered.

A long blink shielded his eyes, and something like disappointment flitted along the lines of his face before he swallowed and opened his eyes, searching. "How many guys have you been with?"

Embarrassment flashed over my skin, spread over my chest and onto my face.

I averted my gaze.

Why was he doing this to me? We talked so much, most often casually, though at times those conversations turned serious, delving into deeper subjects as we learned more and more about the other. It had always felt like a comfort to have someone to confide in.

But we'd never talked about this.

"Hey," he murmured, his tone shifting, the softness in his voice coaxing me to look back up at him. "You know all about me."

Christian lifted one hand, the grimaced smile on his face almost pained, and counted off with his fingers. "Six, twenty-two, or maybe seventy-four."

They were like little contemptuous checkmarks lifted in the air. "I can't count that high, remember?" he said. "I'm bound to lose track."

He was clearly trying to make light of it, but the words held a distinct undertone of hurt. "Don't you think it's fair if I know a little bit about you?"

I blew out a slow breath, remembering how I'd put him on the spot before. Friends would know this about each other, anyway, but he and I both knew this wasn't about us being friends.

"Just one," I finally said, dipping my head down and to the side to hide the redness I knew would be there, though I couldn't help but slant my eyes to watch his reaction. "He was my boyfriend for three years."

I hated the heaviness that crept over me when I thought of Ryan, hated more that Christian had more of an effect on me than Ryan ever had.

"Of course, because I was fifteen and naïve when we started dating, I thought he was the one."

A bitterness I'd kept concealed for too long broke loose. "He bugged me our entire senior year until I finally gave in right before graduation. I had sex with him three times and all three times were awful. Then he broke up with me. That's it."

I shrugged nonchalantly, playing it off as if I hadn't just divulged the entirety of my pitiful experience with guys and that I hadn't been a fool to fall for this obvious exploitation.

I was pinned to the chair by Christian's sudden severity. My chest squeezed as his head tilted just to the side, the depths of that place I was scared to tread exposed.

"Do you still love him?"

I fumbled through the emotions Christian had crashing around inside of me for an answer, unable to discern how I felt. I licked my lips to steady myself.

When I spoke, my voice trembled. "No. I mean, it still hurts because of what he did. I was devastated for about a week, but it wasn't hard to realize we didn't have a future together. I just wish he would have broken up with me before he had sex with me. I can't stop thinking about how stupid I was falling for it."

"And the asshole didn't even know how to take care of you," Christian murmured, the assertion rough and abraded.

His eyes were a destructive force as he stared at me.

There was no questioning what Christian was thinking right then.

A lump grew in my throat, the air between us too thick to swallow.

"You have no idea how badly I want to track down that guy and make him pay for what he did to you . . . for treating you that way."

His words knocked me back from the physical response flooding my body. I frowned at him. "How is that any different than what you do?"

He blinked a couple times and hefted the air from his lungs. Our faces were so close, I felt it rush across my face. "Maybe there's no difference . . . I don't know . . ."

He angled a hand through his hair and down the back of his neck. "But I've never told anyone I loved them or that I wanted to be with them so they'd have sex with me. I can't tell you how angry it makes me that he did that to you."

A tremor rolled through him, something palpable, more than jealousy.

I knew it then.

He truly did care about me.

This friendship was as real as I felt it was.

Maybe there was more to it. Maybe there was something to this simmering attraction that I didn't know how much longer we could ignore.

But right then, this, him caring about me? It was what mattered.

Christian abruptly withdrew his leg and edged back in his chair.

Because we both understood it. The connection we shared was too important to ruin it by giving into the physical.

I faked a smile. "It's fine . . . really. I'm over it. It was for the best. Believe me."

Time passed so quickly. Before I could make

sense of it, November had come. Along with it, the approaching winter had ushered in a new feel in the air.

Christian had become a mainstay in my life, my closest friend, the one who I felt securest with. He was a comfort that wrapped around my body and spread all the way to my bones whenever he was near.

Out of the corner of my eye, I watched him from where I sat lengthwise on his couch. With my back propped up against the arm and my knees bent, I rested my bare feet on the soft suede of the cushions and balanced my calculus book on my thighs.

Christian's apartment was so much more comfortable than mine, and we'd taken to studying here.

A decent-sized kitchen sat off to the left of the entrance, and the dining nook and living room took up the rest of the open space. Down a small hall to the back was his bedroom and bath.

Where my apartment had one small window over my bed, Christian's apartment was open, two windows in his living room and one in his bedroom, something that felt like a total luxury.

During the day, it was brighter in here, a natural warmth flooding the room as rays of light slanted in from between the buildings on the opposite side of the street.

And at night . . . I loved it here at night. Lights seeped in, boasting the city and everything it had to offer. Horns blared and voices rose from the sidewalk below.

Christian's couch had become my spot, and I relished in it now, snuggled against the plush fabric as I tried to maintain focused on my homework.

He sat on the floor, his legs stretched out beneath the coffee table and his back against the sofa. That head of black hair teased me from where it rested just at the juncture of where I had my knees bent.

Tonight, it was all over the place, sticking up in every direction. His hands continually came up to rush through it as if he were frustrated—probably because he was.

If I wanted to, I could reach out and *touch*, run my fingers through the softness. I could only imagine how his head would tilt back in undeniable pleasure, could almost hear a low rumble emitted from deep within his chest, how the sound would vibrate up my arm and cover me whole.

My hand twitched.

Sometimes that desire was so great I almost gave in to it, but we both always pushed it aside because the friendship we shared was so much greater than any fleeting attraction could ever be.

"I'm never going to get this," he mumbled.

"Yes, you will. You always do."

We studied together almost every night, but it wasn't uncommon for us to get distracted, many times talking into the deep hours of the night about everything and anything.

While we were so much the same, there was also so much between us that was different—the way we looked at life and our goals for the future. Streaks of selfishness were so blatantly obvious in some of Christian's words, the things he would say that would take me aback, reminding me of how distinctly different we were.

But here in this place, with Christian on the floor and me on his couch, those things couldn't touch us. I settled into that safety, this place that was ours, where Christian was comfortable enough to put all those pretenses aside.

Christian groaned again, and his head dropped back onto my leg. He cut his blue eyes my direction. "Seriously, this sucks ass."

"What sucks?" I trained my attention on my book in front of me and kept writing, pretending I didn't love the way he felt against me.

That I didn't savor in the slight pressure that slipped through my jeans and caressed my skin, that I didn't love the sound of his voice even when it projected the most ridiculous words.

I already knew what was coming.

"This class sucks, is what." A mischievous grin lighted at the edge of his lips. "Seriously, when do they think we're ever going to use any of this garbage? It's a complete waste of time."

I laughed and nudged him with my leg.

His body rocked a little then settled farther against mine.

"Don't you know that's what college is about . . . students spending years gathering useless information they'll never use again, going hopelessly into debt, just so they feel smarter than the rest of their family? I mean, that's why I worked so hard to get here, anyway."

Sarcasm rolled off my tongue. He was such a whiner. For being one of the smartest guys I knew, he sure found a way to complain about every subject, every night.

I subtly rolled my eyes.

Clearly, he liked the sound of his voice as much as I did.

One side of his mouth tipped up with the cutest smile. It perfectly matched the tilt of his head.

"Fine, it's not *useless*." He reached up and pinched my thigh. "But right now, I can't think of a single time in my life when I'm going to use it."

A vain attempt was made at ignoring the heat spreading up my leg. "Quit complaining. You're going to kick ass at Trivial Pursuit."

This time he really laughed. It vibrated through the cushions and crawled across my skin. I tried to hold in the smile, tried to memorize the way it made me feel.

From the top of the coffee table, the sharp ring of Christian's phone sliced into the room.

Of course, Christian's phone rang constantly. I was never so blunt to ask who was calling.

I found I'd rather not know if it was some girl on the line.

The truth was, I didn't want to know anywhere he went or what he did once he walked me back to my apartment each night. He had no obligation to me, but that didn't mean I could stomach knowing who he was running off to jump in bed with the second I was out of his sight.

Glancing at the screen, he lifted his face to the ceiling and exhaled heavily. "Great," he mumbled.

He reluctantly accepted the call. "Hello."

These were the only times when I paid attention, when I turned my ear to the conversation happening beside me.

I couldn't help but listen when the calls he received caused Christian's shoulders to sag and sucked his light from the room.

I was disgusted by it.

His parents' pressures were so ingrained in him, they held him hostage in a place I was sure Christian didn't even know he was a prisoner.

Every time they called, it was the same.

They never took the time to ask how he was, but rather questioned what he had done, what he had achieved, and pushed him some more.

I'd slowly begun to hate them, resenting them for forcing their son toward something that was so obviously holding him back. Christian insisted this was what he wanted for his life, and I knew part of him truly did want to be an attorney. But I could clearly see striving toward his father's goals for him was more of a burden for Christian than a blessing.

"Hi, Dad."

Through the phone, I could hear his father start right into him. The words might have been muffled, by they were a clear hostile coercion.

"Yeah, I got it."

"No, Dad . . . I already did."

Christian dropped his head, his fingers tugging at the ends of his hair. "I'm doing the best job I can," he said, strained.

"What else do you expect me to do?"

Knots formed in my belly as I listened to the one-sided conversation. As I caught bits of the unfounded criticism and the unjustified berating.

"Fine," Christian mumbled.

"You are?" Surprise increased the volume on those two words, followed by a frustrated sigh.

"Just let me know when and where."

His father ended the call before Christian was given a chance to say goodbye.

It made my heart hurt. I reached out and touched him, my fingers light on his shoulder. This was not giving in. This was being there for my friend.

"Hey."

He didn't respond, just drew his knees up from under the table and wrapped his arms around them. Christian was always larger than life, but right then, he reminded me of a little boy.

"Please don't let them do this to you, Christian. You're amazing, and if they can't see it, then they're completely blind."

The shake of his head was short and buried in his arms.

"Fuck," he groaned on a gravelly breath, rubbing his eyes with the heels of his hands. He cut his gaze over to me with his cheek pressed against his forearm. "I'm going to prove him wrong, Elizabeth. I'm going to be the best damned attorney, and he'll never be able to say another word to me about it."

Worry cinched my lips into a thin line. This was the Christian who scared me the most, the one who couldn't see what his parents were doing to him.

The one who, instead of fighting against it and living for what he wanted, ran head first into it.

Part of me had to understand the desire to please the ones who cared about us, but I didn't believe Christian's parents had his best interest at heart.

"It doesn't have to be that way, Christian. What about what you want? Is this really it? Killing yourself to be the absolute best in everything you do?"

Lines creased between his eyes, his mouth twisting up in set determination. "I'll do whatever it takes, Elizabeth. Nothing is going to stand in my way."

I closed my eyes to block myself from the hardened expression on his face.

He forced a large breath of air from his lungs. "I don't feel like dealing with this shit tonight. You want to get out of here?"

I looked up to find Christian maneuvering around to stand. It was almost ten, an hour or so earlier than when I usually left his place. Christian would always walk me home, then go and do whatever he did after he left me at my door.

Frowning, I attempted to decipher his intent, because it'd sounded like an invitation. "Where do you want to go?"

"There's a party at my friend Sam's. I have to stop by. His birthday was yesterday, and we're celebrating it tonight."

Oh, no way, no thank you.

I sat up and began gathering my things.

"I'll just go home so you can head over," I said with feigned indifference. This was my safe place, the place where it was just Christian and me. I didn't venture into his other world, the one that lit up his phone every weekend. "I'm pretty tired, anyway."

Christian reached out as if he wanted to touch me and then thought better of it.

"I'd . . . would you just come?" The hard lines were gone, sincere blue eyes in their place. "I don't feel like going over there by myself tonight."

Dropping my chin, I bit at my lip as he waited for an answer. Truly, I didn't want to go, didn't want to stray from the comfort zone we'd erected around us, but I didn't know how to resist him when he looked at me like that.

I glanced down at my old T-shirt and faded jeans. "I'm not really dressed to go out."

"We'll stop by your place on the way so you can change and leave your stuff there." He grinned. "And it's not like you could ever look bad, Elizabeth."

I rolled my eyes at him, hating the little flutter that palpitated my heart whenever he said things like that. We both knew flattery was really unnecessary since it was obvious he had already talked me into it.

"Fine."

I gathered my stuff, slipped into my jacket, and hefted my backpack onto my shoulders. I followed Christian out and down his hall.

He pulled open the stairwell door and extended

his arm to hold it open, though he remained in front of me, as if he might need to catch me if I were to trip and fall.

The stairwell always seemed much too tight, the walls like a barrier that held in all the energy that radiated between us.

Outside the air was crisp, the night alive. I breathed it in, hoping to quell my racing nerves.

I could do this.

Christian was my friend, and it wasn't fair for me to avoid every other aspect of his life that didn't involve me. I'd made it clear before that I wanted to know him, really know him, and how could I if the only time I spent with him was behind his apartment door?

His hands were shoved in his pockets, his stride strong but slowed to sync with mine as he walked alongside me.

"So . . ." He breathed out, puffing out his cheeks as he did. "Turns out my parents are coming here for Thanksgiving after all."

"Really? Is that what your dad called about?" I lifted a brow. Originally, his parents were supposed to be out of the country for the holiday. "You sound thrilled about it."

Sarcasm arched my brow.

An incredulous sound slipped from his mouth. "A perfect night in Hell . . . Thanksgiving dinner at some stuffy restaurant with my dad harassing me the entire time. *Can't wait.*"

We walked a couple steps in silence before Christian fixed his gaze on me. "Why don't you come with me?"

Laughter bubbled up at the absurdity, but I held it in when I realized he remained silent, waiting.

Oh.

He was serious.

I frowned.

This sounded like a really bad idea. I couldn't stand his parents, and I hadn't even met them yet. "Don't you think that's a little bit weird? I mean, won't they get the wrong idea or something?"

"Maybe." A small shrug of his shoulders discounted it. "But I don't really care. Let them think whatever the hell they want. I just don't want to go by myself, and I don't want you sitting at home by yourself on Thanksgiving, either. At least if you're there, my dad will lay off me a little. He wouldn't want to look like the asshole he is in front of someone he doesn't know."

"So what you're saying is you want me to protect you from your parents?" I teased.

"Exactly." He knocked into me, jostling my body slightly to the side, the weight gone from his face as he laughed. "No, Elizabeth, you're my best friend. Who else would I want to spend Thanksgiving with?"

His words struck me, and I warmed from head

to toe. That was really all I needed. I slowed to the point of barely walking, and I turned completely to face Christian at my side. "You're my best friend, too, Christian. You know that, right?"

He didn't say anything. He didn't need to. The expression on his face said it all.

He was all sweet and adoring, that soft look that always warned how easily we could slip.

Fall.

I drew in a deep breath and turned ahead.

"So? You're coming?" he prodded as I stepped in front of him to open my building door.

"Of course, I'll come."

He followed me inside and up the stairs. "Guess I managed to talk you into two things you didn't want to do tonight."

He was so close behind me, his breath rustled through my hair.

"Um, yeah . . . I guess you did."

"Must be my lucky night."

I glanced over my shoulder at the smirk I already knew would be waiting there. The lightness in his tone warned me he'd made the flip to that cocky boy I'd met the first time in the café. I figured I'd be dealing with him all night since we were heading over to his friends', although I wasn't entirely sure what to expect.

I played along, smirked back. "Yeah, I'm sure it will be. Let's see what little tramp you end up ditching me for tonight. Do you prefer blondes or brunettes?"

Laughter rang out and ricocheted on the brick walls, a thunder that pounded in my chest.

He reached out and tugged on a strand of my hair. "Blondes, Elizabeth. Blondes. And did you just say tramp?"

"Yep, sure did."

"Oh, you're going to make all kinds of new friends tonight."

Fifteen minutes later, we were walking side-by-side toward Sam's apartment, a guy I'd never met, but was legendary in the stories Christian told.

Knowing them only managed to make me more nervous than before. I'd changed into my best jeans, a cute, wide-necked sweatshirt, and boots, hoping not to embarrass Christian since he was dragging me along.

I was never one for parties. Maybe because to me it symbolized what I'd given up to make it here.

If I were being honest? It just wasn't my scene. The few I'd been to had been uncomfortable. The predatory feel in the air. Guys assessing whether a girl was as easy as she looked, and girls competing to win that attention.

No thanks.

I glanced back down at what I'd changed into, pretty sure I was going to be completely out of place. With longing, I glanced behind me. Maybe I could come up with an excuse, turn around, and go home so I could crawl in my little bed and hide.

"I'm really glad you decided to come with me."

I jerked my head back to Christian. He flashed me an all-knowing grin, as if he knew exactly what I'd been thinking.

"Yeah, me, too," I blatantly lied.

Christian chuckled, lifted his face to the night sky with a satisfied breath pushed out into the air. He appeared so relaxed, so casual as he ambled along.

I followed as if there was nowhere else for me to go.

We turned right at the intersection, and Christian grabbed my hand. I sucked in a sharp breath and tried to hide the way the simple gesture made me feel.

His hand was warm, perfect, felt too right.

He tugged me to his side. "This is it."

My eyes traveled the height of the building. It was much nicer than mine, but not nearly as nice as Christian's.

Ten stories of lit windows lined the building. Energy radiated from its walls. Nerves hit me again as Christian swung the door open, and they eased just as quickly when he squeezed my hand.

What was he doing to me tonight?

He had my emotions all over the place. I'd come

to feel so comfortable in his presence, the want inside had subdued to a peaceful glow. It had come into something that felt like a stronger connection, something I could control.

Tonight . . . I wasn't sure. Something had shifted, tilted the axis where I thought I'd found a perfect balance.

He led me down a narrow hall and pressed the button to the elevator. An encouraging smile lifted his mouth when he looked down at me. "Don't be nervous. Everyone's really nice."

A slight chuckle echoed in the confines of the old elevator when we stepped inside, and still he held my hand, a gentle encouragement, maybe a thank you for coming. "I mean, they're idiots, but nice."

I nodded subtly.

Great.

The elevator door slid open on the fifth floor. Music pumped into the hall from behind what seemed like every door.

Several doors down the hall, Christian rapped twice and swung it open without an invitation.

He towed me in behind him. My feet faltered, and I shrank back when I met the scene inside. People littered the room, packed together, the space so full and overbearing that my throat tightened, and I found it hard to breathe.

"Christian!" a guy shouted from across the din

of the room. He wore his hat backward and a wrinkled button-up, his tongued slurred.

"Hey, man."

Christian inclined his head my direction, whisper-shouted in my ear. "That's Tom."

I nodded. Christian had mentioned him before, always in a *you won't believe what my dumbass friend did* sort of way.

"And who do we have here?"

"This is my friend, Elizabeth."

"Elizabeth." The tilt of Tom's head told me he'd heard my name before. He extended his hand. Dark brown eyes shifted down the length of my body as he shook my hand.

I had the urge to hide behind Christian or maybe run.

I looked back around the room again.

Yes. Yes. Running seemed like a really good idea.

"Come on." Christian tugged me into the crowd.

A crush of bodies and music and the overpowering smell of alcohol washed over me in a heady wave.

His mouth was close to my ear. "You want a beer?"

Not really, but what else was I supposed to do in this atmosphere? "Sure," I shouted over the music.

Christian wound us through the room. He paused to talk to a few people, introducing me to faces and names I would never remember. To the right, a small kitchen overflowed with students surrounding a keg. The music played from the other room.

In here, people yelled as they drank. Guys were clearly scoping out who they wanted to take home tonight, the girls laughing too loud and wearing too little.

Self-consciously, I peeked down at my jeans and sweatshirt. No question, I was out of place. It was affirmed by the stares I received, the quick glances and hushed whispers.

I edged closer to Christian's side.

What in the world was he thinking bringing me here?

Strangest was, in it, Christian emanated ease, brash as he bantered with his friends.

It was hard to reconcile the two, the Christian I'd come to know in our quiet evenings at his place and the one I'd first recognized when he walked through the door to the café more than three months before.

Worst was, *they* were here. I could feel them, the eyes that caressed Christian with familiarity, those who'd known his body the way I'd never allow myself to.

Their eyes would ultimately slide to study my

face with barely constrained sneers, then drop to the place where Christian had his hand wrapped around mine.

What they didn't know was that this was the first time Christian had ever held my hand, that I didn't belong to him, and that I never would.

Jealousy struck me like a slap to the face.

Because for the most fleeting moment, I wished for once to trade them places. For just once to slip into the role of the casual girl who could handle *this*.

Christian broke from me, filled a red cup, and passed it my direction, cutting into my thoughts. His smile was so infectious, directed only at me. Blue eyes embraced my face, searching, silently asking if I was okay.

I'd once thought him too pretty.

Now I knew better.

He was beautiful.

I'd spent countless days and hours with him, and the effect was still the same.

I'd just learned to disguise it, to lump it in with the affection I felt for him as a friend. And it was strong, the part of me that begged for Christian's touch. But the affection I held for him was so much greater than the hunger these girls were watching him with, so much greater than the obscured lust that swirled and pulsed in my veins.

That was why I could never give into one night.

Not even a short-lived affair. It just wasn't worth it. I'd never survive without Christian in my life.

Sipping at the bitter liquid in my cup, I fidgeted uncomfortably as my attention flitted around the room at the faces of the people Christian called friends.

Halfheartedly, I listened to the conversations happening around me, pretending to act as if I was interested and enjoying myself since Christian seemed to be having fun.

I forced myself to finish one beer in the span of time it took Christian to down five.

He attempted to include me, but I just couldn't settle. Couldn't find comfort in this place.

Yanking at the hem of his shirt to get his attention, I tried to keep the discomfort out of my expression when he turned back to me.

"Is there a restroom I can use?" I asked.

No doubt, he was a little buzzed, his pupils wider and slowed. Squinting, he focused on me. Then he tipped me that earth-shattering smile. "Yeah, sure . . . it's right down the hall. You want me to come with you?"

I forced myself to smile back. "No, I'm fine. I'll be right back."

"Okay." He turned back to the guy he was talking to.

Keeping my head down, I made my way through the crowd, twisting and turning as I did my best to avoid both eye and skin contact.

I fumbled my way through as if I were lost in a jungle and searching for escape.

Thank God the bathroom was empty.

I shut the door behind me and leaned against it. Raising my face to the ceiling, I expelled a weighted sigh into the reprieve of the bathroom. Music vibrated through the walls, though it was dimmed and dulled.

What the hell am I doing?

It was ridiculous to feel this much discomfort. It wasn't like I wasn't surrounded by these same kinds of people in my classes, that I didn't sit by them every day, or that I really thought bad about any of them.

The most unsettling part was that I wasn't normally this insecure girl who cared about prying eyes or what anyone thought of me.

Awareness pressed into my senses.

I refuted it.

Internally denied it.

But its truth screamed in my ear.

An unfound possessiveness rapid fired from my nerves, spun and wove a web around my heart, and the jealousy I'd felt earlier beat a steady song within the confines of my chest.

I forced myself to move to the sink and splashed cool water on my face. It struck me again, and I gripped my hands in my hair.

Shit. Shit. Shit.

I was never supposed to allow myself to feel this way.

Straightening, I looked up at the misery that awaited me in the mirror.

What the hell was I supposed to do now?

Someone banged at the door. "Come on . . . you're not the only person here."

Sighing, I steeled myself and headed out, ducking my head when I was met with the scowl on the face of the girl waiting on the other side of the door.

"About time."

I didn't acknowledge her, just brushed by with my attention trained on the ground. The hall was dark as I hauled myself forward and worked my way back through the throng.

All I wanted was to find Christian and ask him to get me out of here.

A foreign hand pulled at my arm as I passed, and I spun around to one of the guys Christian had introduced me to when we first got here.

Max?

Yes, that was it.

Max.

"Where you goin' so fast?"

Panic stretched tight across my chest, and I yanked my arm away, hating his obvious perusal and my reaction to it. "I'm looking for Christian."

"Of course, you are. Just like everyone else." The guy laughed in his stupor. "Well, if you can't find him, you know where to find me."

Ugh.

Why was Christian so into this?

Pushing forward, I came to a stumbling standstill on the outskirts of the living room.

Because I knew why. I always had.

Christian had moved into the living room. Even from here, he crowded my space.

His presence slipped over my skin, penetrating, invading everything. He held me in a way no one ever had, in a way I knew was impossible for anyone else to.

He leaned with one shoulder on the wall while some girl with long brown hair nearly climbed his body, inching up to whisper something in his ear. His head tilted back, and I caught a flash of his gorgeous face before he leaned back into her.

This.

This was why he was here.

An ache unlike anything I'd ever felt pierced me.

All the way to the core.

I wasn't angry with Christian. He'd never tried to hide this from me. Had never lied and had never promised me anything. And the little he'd asked me for, I'd immediately shot down.

It didn't mean seeing him here, like this, didn't hurt like I'd been thrown into the deepest, most excruciating pit in Hell.

I couldn't be here.

Couldn't witness this.

Not when it hurt so much.

Turning, I fled, shoving through the throbbing crowd. Mumbles and annoyed stares met me on all sides.

I couldn't find it in myself to care.

Not with the knot of agony that had found its way inside of me.

Forcing them out of the way, I tore out the door, wanting so desperately to look back but knowing I couldn't handle what I would see.

I had to get out there. Erase this night and the images it had created.

The feelings it had summoned.

I didn't bother to wait for the elevator.

Instead, I grappled with the metal latch and flung the stairwell door open wide. My footsteps pounded on the cement stairs and echoed in my ears.

Labored breaths panted from my mouth.

With burdened feet, I stumbled outside. Cool air clashed with my flaming skin, and I bent over and tried to catch my breath.

Gasping.

Stupid, stupid girl.

I'd been a fool for allowing this to happen.

I pulled out my phone, typed out the easiest

excuse I could find, and pressed send.

Then I ran from the one thing in my life I wanted most.

CHRISTIAN

I tried to ignore the way I felt when Elizabeth left

my side to find the restroom, but it was impossible. I downed the rest of my beer, hoping it'd cover the sudden void inside that told me I was missing something.

"Dude, you wouldn't believe how fucking funny it was. You should have been there."

Kenny leaned in close to my ear so I could hear him tell the story about a girl he'd seen crash into three different cars in a parking lot when he'd ventured into New Jersey the weekend before. "She had to be the dumbest bitch I've ever seen in my life."

I struggled to pay attention. To smile and laugh along.

But my only focus was this strange sensation.

How my hand burned from the first true contact I'd ever had with Elizabeth.

I'd taken her hand to give her reassurance because she was all jerky with nervous energy, as if we were getting ready to enter the place where her worst nightmares were bred.

It was just to give her a little comfort. A simple gesture to remind her I was there.

Then it turned out, I was the one who couldn't let go. I was only holding her hand, for fuck's sake, and now it was all I could think about.

I felt singed from the inside out, or maybe the outside in, I couldn't really tell.

It was all encompassing.

I was beginning to think the resolution I'd made months before was a mistake, because I was hard just from holding a girl's hand.

I really needed to get laid.

Truth was, Elizabeth was slowly driving me insane.

Physically.

Emotionally.

Completely.

The urge to reach out and touch her again was killing me. To run my fingers across her face and over her lips. To push it further.

To push *her* further.

To end this madness that had me spun up, teetering at the cusp, so close to spinning me out of control.

Everything had been great for the last couple of months.

Perfect, really.

We spent so much time together, I'd almost become accustomed to the physical ache she left burning inside me. The hardest part was pretending that it didn't build, that each time I opened the door to find Elizabeth's face smiling up at me in my doorway, I didn't come one step closer to snapping.

That my heart didn't want to burst at the sight of her and my body didn't scream for her to run her delicate hands all over me.

So many times, I'd had to stop myself from reaching out.

Touching her.

Taking her.

Living out every single one of the fantasies that played through my mind at night.

In them, I'd had her everywhere, in my bed, the shower, the floor, time and time again on my couch where she sat and unwittingly teased and taunted me night after night.

Tonight was proof of just how close I was

coming to the edge.

"They finally got her out of the car, and this girl was standing there, stumbling all over the place in these slutty heels," Kenny continued on.

Why was I here again? Listening to this? Usually, I liked to be here, to unwind, to listen to trivial stories that meant nothing.

But with Elizabeth here, it felt like a weakness.

A fool's waste of time.

Glancing back out the entryway, my eyes traveled the crowd.

Elizabeth had only been gone a couple seconds, but I couldn't shake this nagging feeling that I shouldn't have let her out of my sight.

It was stupid to bring her here, but there was no way I could sit in the confines of my apartment after listening to my father's bullshit.

I was sick of it.

I'd thought that once I moved out and started college—started my own *life*—my father would let up and let go. But he was just as overbearing as he'd been since I was a little boy.

A tyrant who expected only the best, something he made quite clear I didn't ever have a chance of living up to.

Besides for that, I'd already committed to coming here tonight. I didn't want to the asshole who bailed last minute. But there'd been no chance I could stomach the idea of leaving Elizabeth alone in front of her building tonight.

Somehow when she was around, I felt . . . *better*.

I needed her.

Tom appeared at my side and clapped me on the shoulder. The guy was trashed, which was no surprise. I smirked at him. "What's up?"

"So you finally let Elizabeth out to play." He cocked his head to the side in the direction where Elizabeth had disappeared, suggestion written all over his face. "Now I get why you've been hiding from us the last couple of months . . . or where you've been hiding. That shit is hot."

A swell of protectiveness broke over me. My fists curled, but I forced the reaction down. "It's not like that."

"So you wouldn't mind if I went for her?"

"Yeah, I'd fucking mind. She's my best friend. Do you think I'm going to let some asshole like you touch her?"

Tom laughed, not for a second offended.

"Your best friend, huh? Thought that was my title." His eyes gleamed as he razzed me, a clear insinuation he'd been hinting at for months, one I'd continually denied.

"Quit being a dick." I shrugged it off. "We're just friends."

As I said it, I lifted up on my toes, straining to see over the heads littering the room.

Anxiety knocked at my ribs.

Where the hell was she?

If one of these losers even thought about messing with her, I was going to lose it. I wasn't typically a violent guy, but I was pretty sure bones would get broken.

I rushed an uneasy hand through my hair, hoping for calm.

Stupid.

Reckless to bring her here.

I looked back at Tom who was staring at me with straight-out disbelief.

Then he cracked up, loud and raucous. "You, my friend, are completely fucked. You might as well give it up because I don't believe a word you're saying. Pretty sure you don't, either."

He was still laughing when he walked away.

I made the conscious decision to ignore him and the implications of his words. I moved into the main room and leaned against the wall so I could watch for Elizabeth.

Dimness hung to the room, the faces cast in shadows.

Sam's apartment was always primed for the perfect party.

Loud music pounded in my ears, the feel chaotic as bodies moved. Fuzziness eddied around my vision, and with both palms, I scrubbed my face to clear it, wishing I'd have thought better than to have drank so much with Elizabeth being here tonight.

Disquiet gripped me tight.

I couldn't help it.

She was here with me.

My responsibility.

It was more than that, though.

The thought of anyone looking at her, let alone touching her, sent a swirl of nausea thrashing through my already raw stomach. But how could I claim her when I didn't even trust myself with her?

I cared about her.

A lot.

The problem was, I knew myself too well, the fleeting interest that passed just as quickly as it came. I refused to lose my best friend to my own stupidity and selfishness.

But God, this was getting unbearable.

A hand wrapped around my wrist before a hot body flattened against my side.

"There you are."

Locks of dark brown hair obstructed my view, pushed into my space. Every weekend, it was the same.

Irritation had me shaking my head. "What do you want, Rachel?"

She pouted before she stretched up on her toes to whisper in my ear. "You."

Jerking my head back, I glared at her, unable to fathom how one girl could be so clueless. "Haven't

I turned you down enough?"

She ran a single fingertip down the length of my face.

I recoiled.

"One of these days, you'll be begging me."

That wasn't going to happen. She had to be the most disgusting slut I knew.

A few months ago, I might not have minded.

Maybe.

Even then, I had some discretion. But now? Not a chance. Just the thought of her touching me had my skin crawling.

"The only thing I'm begging you for is to leave me alone."

"Whatever. Your loss."

Rachel walked away, still looking at me over her shoulder, like somehow the exaggerated sway of her hips would send me chasing after her. She blended in with the mob, lost in the jumble.

With her out of the way, my attention jumped from one person to the next, searching for the only face I wanted to see.

A tremor of agitation rolled through my muscles. I flexed my fists and shook it off.

Shouldn't she be out by now?

I couldn't tell how much time had passed, and again, I wished I'd been wiser and not drank so much. Really, I wished I wouldn't have brought her with me at all.

Elizabeth didn't belong here.

She was too good. Too pure.

Unable to wait any longer, I weaved through the room, ignoring everyone who tried to talk to me as I headed down the hallway. The bathroom door was closed. I jingled the knob. When I found it locked, I pounded on the bathroom door.

"Elizabeth? Are you in there?" I shouted against the wood, listening for movement inside.

A female voice yelled back, "Not Elizabeth. It's Kim."

"Shit," I mumbled under my breath.

Pulling back, I looked to the opposite end of the hall to the single bedroom I knew would be locked. That was the one place in Sam's apartment that was off limits.

She had to have slipped by me, probably had some guy salivating all over her when she got back and didn't find me there.

Panic ratcheted up inside of me as I rushed back toward the main room.

I found Sam standing at the end of the hall, talking with Max. I tapped him on the shoulder. "Hey, have you seen Elizabeth?"

He spun around to look at me. The frantic way the question fell from my mouth did nothing to counter the earlier assertion he'd made.

He drew his brow together and shrugged. "Nah, man, I haven't seen her since before I talked to you."

My frenzied gaze probed the room again, my hands shaking as I dragged them both through my hair.

Max laughed beside me. "You shouldn't have let that one out of your sight."

I speared him to the floor with my eyes. He visibly shrank back without moving an inch, his tone shifting. "She was looking for you about five minutes ago."

Shoving through the bodies, I searched, something akin to fear pulsing through my veins. I didn't understand it—the tightness in my chest, this gripping worry tangling with the desire Elizabeth had left me with when she walked away.

The room felt too confined, and I forced my way through the crowd, pushing and shoving and basically being a total dick.

But every second spurred something higher in me.

Faces glared at me in irritation. I didn't even stop to apologize.

Elizabeth was nowhere in the living room. The kitchen was jammed with people, all except the one I was so desperate to find.

Frustration bubbled up. I wanted to scream.

Fuck.

I dug into my pocket to find my phone to call her. The little red light flashed.

I opened it to a message from Elizabeth. Relief slammed me. Thank God.

That was until I read what she'd texted.

Elizabeth: Sorry. Tired. Will CU later.

The worry I felt transformed and lifted. A throb of anger formed a lump in my throat.

What the hell?

She just left. Without saying a word.

Why would she do this to me? Did she have any idea how fucking worried I was about her?

I dialed, but it went straight to voicemail, her phone deadened. That only managed to piss me off more.

Pushing through the crowd and out the door, I stumbled into the empty hallway. I glanced at the illuminated lights on the elevator. The car was higher in the building.

Unwilling to wait, I took stairs, propelled by anger and confusion, all wrapped up in a cloak of anxiety that something might happen to Elizabeth as she walked home by herself.

What was she thinking?

In all the months Elizabeth and I had hung out, she'd never once pulled anything like this.

Reliable.

Thoughtful.

That was Elizabeth.

But what? She was fucking tired so she walked home by herself in the middle of the night? Without telling me first?

Cold air jolted my senses as I stepped outside. Crowds still coursed the sidewalk. Couples roamed, and groups headed to wherever they were going that night.

My head whipped to the left in the direction of her apartment.

She was already gone.

I started out a flat-out run. Dodging people and barely pausing before I raced across the intersections.

I was panting by the time I stood outside her building. Pausing for a split second, I glanced up to the second floor and saw her light blazing through her window.

She was there.

Anger and relief. They cut a path through my insides.

Flinging open the building door, I barreled up the stairs. Frustration and something that felt a whole lot like hurt ebbed out the worry. Five seconds later, I was pounding on her door. I shuffled my feet impatiently, knocked again when she didn't answer after a couple of seconds.

Finally, movement stirred on the other side of the door, and I could feel her peering out at me from the peephole.

Metal slid as she released the lock, and Elizabeth cracked open the door.

Confusion and sadness saturated the visible half of her face.

I bit back the urge to yell at her and forced down the anger when I saw the affliction twisting up the corner of her mouth.

I blinked, trying to make sense of what had happened in the span of ten minutes.

"Elizabeth." It was a plea. *What did I do?*

Because I knew she wouldn't have left without saying goodbye simply because she was tired.

"What are you doing here?" she asked, averting her timid gaze to the ground.

"What do you mean, what am I doing here? I was worried about you."

I nudged open the door.

Elizabeth staggered back a couple of feet. Everything about her was beaten down. Blonde waves fell around her saddened face.

My fingers twitched, wishing to push it back, to force her to look at me.

"What happened?"

"I just . . ." She shook her head as she slowly lifted her eyes to find mine. Sadness pooled in the depths. "I don't know anymore, Christian."

That feeling washed over me again, something that resembled pain, something foreign that made it hard to breathe.

I stepped forward and dipped my head to capture her attention. I couldn't stand for her to look away from me. "Did I do something wrong?"

Cold, quiet laughter rumbled from her throat. "No, Christian."

She raised both shoulders before she dropped them in defeat. "I felt out of place there, okay? I'm sorry I just took off, but I don't fit into that world, and I guess I didn't really feel comfortable seeing you in it, either."

I pushed a strained breath from my lungs. The sound hung in the air between us. "I'm sorry, Elizabeth. I shouldn't have taken you there."

Her discomfort had been obvious, the way she continually fidgeted, her shy eyes downcast as she stood beside me.

Maybe it'd been selfish of me because I'd only been concerned about how good it felt having her standing by my side, that having her there had given me a valid excuse to relish in her soft skin against mine. Maybe I liked the way all the girls looked on her with envy. Maybe for a few minutes, I liked pretending we were more than what we really were.

Pretending was safe.

"I just wanted to hang out with you."

Elizabeth shrugged like it didn't matter and turned back to whatever she was cooking on the stove. She'd taken off her boots and jeans and had changed into these tight little gray leggings that showed off every perfect curve of her body.

Barefoot, she stirred the pot, stirring something inside of me. I probably should have tried to stop them, but my thoughts went straight back to earlier.

To how good her simple touch had felt.

The burn.

I suppressed a groan.

God, why did she have this effect on me? She was my best friend, and all I wanted to do right then was bury myself inside her.

For hours.

Again and again.

I pushed down the unwelcomed lust. Now was not the time for it. Instead, I waited for the response I could feel Elizabeth working up to.

Slowly, she rocked while I watched her from behind. One hand gripped the pot handle while she gentled the spoon through the soup with the other, her head tilted to one side.

My gaze traveled the flawless span of her body.

Swallowing, she straightened, her hair swishing across her back. She released an audible sound of distress, and she seemed to have to force her voice through it. "Didn't you want to stay there?"

Honesty flowed from my mouth in a soft whisper. "No . . . not if you're not there."

It was true. There wasn't anyone I'd rather be

with.

"But . . ." Elizabeth trailed off, a heavy implication seeded in the word.

My steps were slow as I crept up behind her. I stopped an inch of my chest brushing her back. Everything closed in around us, as if the small space separating us no longer existed. "But what?"

If I wasn't paying such close attention, I would have missed the way her muscles tensed, the subtle flinch as she dropped her head.

"I saw you with that girl." Her admission flooded from her mouth as a trembled whisper, and swells of resentment emanated from her body, rushed in waves across mine, her shallow breaths distinct in the otherwise silent room.

Elizabeth was jealous.

A selfish satisfaction permeated my being, and something overpowering rose up in the pit of my stomach.

It was wrong, but unstoppable.

Over the last few months, she'd done her best to hide her attraction. But I'd seen it, found it in the way she looked at me when she thought I wasn't paying attention.

How her eyes would roam and skim, spurring a tension between us that slowed our movements.

Every time, it would feel like the air in the room had been compressed.

In those moments, I'd glimpsed in her what I'd

been trying to hold back in myself since the second I'd seen her.

But this . . . I wondered if she felt anything close to what I felt when she'd admitted to me a month ago that she'd slept with some guy. That someone had touched her.

Possessive envy had roiled through my veins, and I couldn't tell what I wanted more—to kill this guy for what he'd done to her or show her how good I could make her feel.

"Elizabeth . . ." I leaned in close to one side of her shoulder, my mouth near her ear. "Did you really think I would ditch you for Rachel?"

How could she possibly think that?

"She's all over me every weekend, and I've never even touched her. You can't just take off because you assume something is going on when you have no idea what's really happening. Do you think I'm such a jerk that I'd take you to that party and then leave with Rachel?"

My voice softened. "You *scared* me."

The last came with the residual of my fear. Yeah. I wanted her. But she had to know it went so much deeper than that.

I cared about her so damned much and wouldn't know what I'd do if anything ever happened to her.

I saw the remorse in the sag of her shoulders.

"Elizabeth—"

"No. I don't think that. I just . . ." she mumbled. "I'm sorry."

Waves fell to one side, a gentle sway of her body that I matched. Her wide-collared shirt had slipped off the cap of her delicate shoulder, teasing me with the honey-kissed skin. Her movements were all innocent and sad.

I had the sudden, overwhelming need to mark her.

Claim her.

I descended on her before I could stop myself, my mouth gentle as I kissed her below the slope where her neck and shoulder met, my hands firm on her hips.

She tasted like heaven.

My entire body hardened as I pressed myself along the length of her back.

For a moment, Elizabeth melted, a supple yielding as her head lolled to the side in a second's submission before she froze and spun to untangle herself from my hold.

Lines forged a path of betrayal across her face, and tears gathered in her eyes. "What are you doing?"

I stumbled back, my body still reeling from its first taste of Elizabeth. And all I could think was I wanted more.

Our chests heaving, we just stared, lost in desire and indecision.

"Elizabeth," I breathed across the space.

Her eyes flashed with the sound of her name.

I couldn't stop this, whatever insanity she had brought over me. I inched back toward her, raised my hand, and caressed my fingers down her cheek.

Her eyes fell closed and her lips parted.

My hand slid around to palm her neck, while I wove the other arm around her waist. I tipped her head up at the same time as I pulled her flush against me. The fire I'd kept inside for so many months licked at my insides, seeking a way out.

Elizabeth gasped and her eyes flew open. The honeyed amber liquefied, her expression so soft and unsure. Shaky hands came up to rest on my chest.

She wanted me as badly as I wanted her.

I knew it, could feel it as a tremor rolled down her spine and spread out beneath my palms. I didn't know how to handle this, had no idea what I felt other than how fucking amazing she felt wrapped up in my arms.

I searched for hesitation, but all I found was her willing me to do it.

To cross the line she'd put in place.

I dipped down and pressed my mouth to hers. With just the slightest touch, desire ripped through me, spiked in a place I'd never felt before.

The hands on my chest fisted in my shirt, and Elizabeth lifted up on her toes.

Needing to get closer.

My head spun as I intensified the kiss. My mouth became desperate as I moved against the sweetness of her lips, coaxing, begging.

A tiny moan vibrated up her throat, and Elizabeth surrendered. Her mouth opened, and our tongues met in an eruption that had been building for too many months.

I could almost taste her inexperience.

She explored my mouth so tentatively, as if she were seeking something without knowing what she was looking for, telling me something when she didn't have the words.

Indistinct murmurings melted as they met my lips. I swallowed them down, kissed her deeper. Fingers threaded through my hair, and she gently tugged to bring me closer.

A thrill shot through my body.

"Elizabeth," I murmured at her mouth, pulling away for the smallest second to anchor my fingers in her hair, to look at this girl I still couldn't understand—one who scared me yet made me so insanely happy all at the same time.

My fingers spread out, and I held her head in both hands.

She lifted her face to me.

Nothing had ever felt like this, this need that coiled and pooled and pulsed.

I needed her. Needed her in a way I'd never

needed anything in my life.

I captured her mouth again, and I dropped one hand and smoothed it over her shoulder and down her side.

Chills shot through Elizabeth, and she shook as I snaked my hand just under the hem of her sweatshirt. My thumb teased across the bare flesh at her hip, testing how far she wanted this go.

Elizabeth only nipped at my lip and tugged it between her teeth.

I almost lost it. The ache I'd been dealing with for months multiplied and transformed.

"Oh shit, Elizabeth."

Her bare skin scorched me as I glided my palm up her back. I was met with no barriers, her skin smooth as I explored the soft expanse along the length of her back.

"Christian," she whispered, clutching me just as tightly as I clutched her.

Her fingers dug in deeper, her body imploring. "Christian, I need you."

This girl, my best friend. My best friend. And I knew I was a fool, so stupid to push her. I couldn't stand the thought of losing her, but I couldn't stand the thought of not having her, either.

I didn't want it to end, so I pushed it further and slid my palm around her slim waist. A tiny shudder escaped Elizabeth, and she flexed her stomach as she sucked in a shocked breath.

But she never let go.

The soft ridges of her flat belly enticed me further. My hand jerked as I inched it up. The hand in her hair tightened, and the force of my kiss bowed her back.

Her weight rested on my forearm as I supported her head, my body nearly hovering over hers.

How many times had I imagined this, what it'd be like to touch her?

I skimmed over her small, round breast, my thumb flicking across her nipple.

Elizabeth whimpered and pushed herself further into my hand, emitted this sound that tickled my ears and spurred me forward.

"Shit . . . Elizabeth," I mumbled, quick to edge her back. Desperate, I pushed her up against the small counter and ground myself into her. Maybe I'd have thought to Elizabeth it'd be the most obscene gesture. Instead, it evoked the most seductive sound to roll from her tongue.

I pulled away for a breath, and Elizabeth searched for air as she lifted her face toward the ceiling. She held onto my shoulders, her chest heaving and her heart thundering.

"Christian . . . I don't . . . please." It was all throaty and warm, discordant, her thoughts as jumbled as mine.

I buried my face in her neck, kissed her down to her collar bone, then up to the hollow behind her ear. Her skin was so sweet and her pants were so thin, and I was consumed by this feeling, too much confusion and disorder and need.

Fuck.

I wanted her, and I felt like I was going crazy because there was no possible way I could get enough of Elizabeth.

A haze surrounded us, desire and lust.

Would she let me? My mouth was at her ear as I bit at her skin, whispered, "Please, Elizabeth, I want to fuck you so bad . . . do you have any idea how badly I want you? Let me inside this sweet body."

My hands traveled to her hips, and my fingertips burrowed into her flesh as I shamelessly pressed myself into her again so she'd make no mistake of what she did to me.

She had to know she was the only one who'd ever done *this* to me, this void she'd created that somehow only she could fill.

Beneath me, Elizabeth froze. Every muscle in her body stiffened before her hands slid from my shoulders to my chest.

She shoved me off her.

Hard.

I was caught off guard, and I floundered back.

Her expression doused me in cold. Extinguished the fire.

Lines of hurt and disgust twisted her face. Silent

tears streamed down her cheeks, and she blinked for the longest moment, before stunned eyes turned up to stare at me.

Shit.

Had that really just come out of my mouth?

My heart pounded too fast, and I tried to catch my breath, to calm my screaming body. I tugged a frustrated hand through my hair. A storm of emotions tore through my consciousness.

"Do you know nothing about me, Christian?" I could see her struggling to hold it in, but more tears fell. "Do you really think that's what I want? To be fucked?"

Just like I knew I would, I hurt her, without even knowing it.

"Is that what this was?" she wheezed, wrapping her arms around her stomach. She took a pained step back. "You came here to fuck me?"

"Elizabeth . . ." I lifted my hand, wishing to reach out and touch her, knowing I couldn't. "That's not what I meant."

"Then what did you mean?" It was an accusation.

I searched for an explanation, how to describe what I felt. I couldn't find the words because I didn't know myself.

A wounded cry worked its way free from Elizabeth, and she squeezed her eyes shut and turned her face down and to the side, hugging herself tighter.

My chest constricted with the need to comfort her, to take her in my arms and just hug her, and tell her we'd work it out, but touching her was what had caused all of this to begin with.

"Elizabeth . . . I—" I didn't know exactly what to say. Wasn't it obvious?

I was dying to have her.

Didn't she get that?

I always had wanted her. But it had grown into something else.

But when she looked back up, I understood it all.

The world dropped from beneath me, and I stumbled back the last few steps until my back was plastered against her door.

My best friend.

Elizabeth's chin quivered, and one side of her mouth was drawn in as if she were chewing on the inside of her lip. But her eyes . . . it was there.

What had I done?

I met her gaze, searching for a mistake, for some way to take it all back to the place where it was just me and Elizabeth. Where we were friends and we laughed and we dealt with all the rest of this shit on the inside.

But I'd crossed the line, and Elizabeth could no longer hold it back.

"Christian," she pled, chancing a tortured step

forward. "Tell me what that was."

I shook my head and swallowed, wishing for an easy escape. I had no idea how to handle this.

Because Elizabeth wanted a promise, and I couldn't give her that. "I don't know . . . I'm sorry, Elizabeth, but I don't know."

She slowly shook her head. "I'm not sure I can do this anymore."

"Don't let this mess up our friendship . . . I can't lose that, Elizabeth."

Disbelief drew her brows together, wove with the sadness in her eyes.

"You don't want to mess up our friendship?" She shook her head. "Just go, Christian."

"Elizabeth . . ."

"Please. It's really late." Deliberating, she twisted her fingers together. "I think I need some time."

Swallowing, I stepped away from the door so I could pull it open. I hesitated but could find nothing to say that would make this any better. All I could think was how much I hated myself for ruining the one truly good thing I had in my life.

With my back to her, I paused, the murmur from my mouth rough. "I really am sorry, Elizabeth."

Then I walked out before I did something else I regretted, quietly clicking the door shut behind me.

seven

ELIZABETH

The sharp click of the door behind me nearly brought me to my knees. I clutched my stomach and struggled to hold in the pain.

But it was too intense.

"Oh, God," I whimpered, holding my palm over my mouth.

There was no stopping the sob from breaking free. It came as an offensive echo around the room.

I wanted to stop it, go back and change it, but it was too late. The damage already done.

I'd stumbled.

Fallen.

Considering how I felt, I should have known better than to let Christian through my door.

At the party, I'd been hit with the magnitude of how deep my affections ran. Wrapped up in how bad that realization stung, it'd left me vulnerable.

The knock on my door had jarred my hopes, flamed the fear, and stoked my need.

I'd hesitated, quieted my breaths, self-preservation kicking in. I'd silently willed him to walk away while my heart begged him to stay.

My rational side had little chance. The second knock beckoned me forward, and I'd peered through the peephole at the man who held me in the palm of his hand.

Fingers shaking, I'd unlocked the door, insecurity slowing my movements as I cracked the door to stare out at Christian.

Lines of anger had twisted his face, and I'd stopped short, confused and sad and relieved. It left me unable to comprehend the conflict he incited in me.

He'd pushed through, and the room had filled with his presence, the air so heavy that I should have seen it as a warning and not as the comfort that came plundering through my senses.

When his warm lips had caressed my neck, it'd almost been too much, and I'd been seconds from surrendering. A panicked voice inside me cried out to stop, to defend my heart, because I was already in far too deep, and I managed to rip myself from the grip I was falling victim to.

I'd spun around with an accusation perched on my lips and stopped dead.

There had been no surfacing from the flood that was Christian Davison because he'd been looking at me as if he felt the same.

Now my body shook and tingled with his residual, this consuming desire coursing through my blood, mingling with this vast depth of misery.

I would have given myself to him.

Offered what I guarded and protected.

Because to me, it was never a game. It was never supposed to be the fumble of a good time.

It was devotion—an act of adoration— something I'd been so foolish to waste before.

It wouldn't have been wasted on Christian. Yet it still would have destroyed me.

I shook my head as I made my way back to the stove, my movements jerky as I flipped off the burner. I shoved the burning pot back to an empty burner.

Anger burned my insides.

God, I felt so angry.

His words had slashed me straight to the core, crushed and cut. They were all the confirmation I needed to know how easily he could devastate me.

Low, mocking laughter tumbled from my

mouth.

He already had . . . because I'd let him.

And I had no idea what I was supposed to do now.

Sleep came in sporadic bouts. I tossed through the daze that tormented the night.

Never had I felt so alone.

New York had once been my fairy tale. Now it felt like a place to escape. Lazy light seeped through the small window, and I rolled to my stomach, trying to press the memories of the night before from my mind.

I didn't want to remember.

I didn't want to feel.

I'd been ignoring my phone all morning. It'd rung at least five times, then bleeped with voicemails that just seemed to break my heart a little more.

When it rang again, I gave up and stretched out to retrieve it from the floor.

It wasn't the number I was expecting, though. Not another apology from Christian that I knew was truly sincere, but still could do nothing to make up for the fact that he didn't feel what I wanted him to.

No.

Instead, it was my older sister.

Still lying in bed, I accepted the call. I tried to clear the roughness from my voice. "Hey, Sarah."

"Are you okay?" she immediately asked.

Apparently, I hadn't done a very good job.

"Yeah, I just woke up."

"Oh . . . sorry for waking you . . . but . . ." Excitement bled through her concern for me. I pictured her bouncing as she stood next to the phone in the small kitchen of the home she'd purchased with her new husband just the year before. "I have some really good news."

I sat up a bit and drew my knees to my chest. Resting one elbow on a knee, I propped my head up in my hand. I forced what I was feeling aside.

Sarah was always so direct, a good listener filled with even better advice, but her mood rarely fluctuated from her mild manner. I knew whatever she'd called to tell me was important.

"What is it?"

"You're going to be an aunt."

Her news shifted through me, wound with the sadness, affixed as a plaintive smile on my lips.

A dense weight welled up inside, filled with both light and heavy.

Distinct happiness laced with what Christian had left me with.

"Oh my gosh, Sarah, I can't believe you're going to be a mom. Are you excited?"

She laughed. "Can't you tell?"

"Um, yeah, I think it's pretty obvious," I said, warmth and joy for her filling my tone.

"So . . ." I hedged, not sure how to phrase it. They'd planned on waiting, establishing their lives and their home before they had children.

I think she expected my unvoiced question. "It was totally an accident, but after the shock wore off, I don't think I've ever been happier."

Her happy sigh was tangible in the distance. Again, I pictured her in her kitchen, but this time with a tender hand resting on her belly.

"I'm so happy for you." I was doing my best at hiding my own turmoil. I didn't want to taint this moment.

Compared to this news, my issues were so trivial.

Still, it was hard to hide it.

"What's going on, Liz?"

"Nothing," I rushed out the obvious lie.

"Don't give me that. You think I can't tell when you're upset?"

My entire family was close, Sarah and I especially so.

Five years older than me, she'd always been my confidant, my defender. She was the one to softly assert she was concerned I might be making a mistake, encouraging me to slow down and think it through, and my biggest supporter whenever I hesitated to try, afraid I would fail.

A strangled groan rose up from my mouth. I flopped with my back to the bed, rubbing my eye with the heel of my hand.

"This has to be about a boy . . . Only a man can make that sound come from a woman."

I knew this was Sarah's attempt at lightening the mood while broaching the subject, but it felt too heavy, too much.

"Is it that Christian guy who always seems to be invading your space every time I talk to you?"

I bit my lip as unwelcomed tears filled my eyes.

"Liz?"

I tried to hold it back, but a choked sob rumbled up and tore from my throat.

Uncontainable.

Unstoppable.

It hurt as it scraped through.

Silence stretched across the line before Sarah finally spoke. "Oh, God, Liz . . . you're in love with him."

It wasn't a question.

It was a statement.

She had this intuition about her. She'd been the one who'd seen through my feelings for Ryan, that as much as I'd illusioned myself with being in love with him, I never had been. I wasn't surprised she could easily tell when I really was.

Hearing those words voiced aloud ripped and tugged, taunted me for being such a fool.

I couldn't blame Christian. This was all on me.

From the start, I'd known what he was like, yet I'd pushed it, invited him into my life. As if that smile wouldn't worm its way into my heart. As if the kindness I saw in the depths of those blue eyes wasn't going to turn me inside out.

Change everything—who I was and what I wanted.

And what I wanted was him.

She remained silent for a few minutes and just let me cry.

"Liz." Sympathy rolled from my sister's tongue, quiet understanding. "I hate that you're all the way over there and I can't hug you right now."

A small jolt of laughter made its way through my tears. "I wish you were here, too. I miss you so much."

Sniffling, I wiped my eyes with the sleeve of my sweatshirt. I rolled to my side and hugged my knees to my chest, held the phone closer to my ear.

"So you want to tell me about it?"

"I don't even know, Sarah. We were just supposed to be friends, and then it was like one day passed, and all of a sudden, I couldn't live without him. Everything was fine until he asked me to go to this party with him last night. I should have known better than to go."

I sucked in a breath. "I hated it there, Sarah. I mean, I can't tell you how it felt to stand in that

141

room and know he's been with half the girls there. I went to the restroom, and when I came out, some girl was rubbing all over him. I couldn't stand it, so I took off without telling him."

"Liz." Disapproval clouded her voice.

"I know, I know. It wasn't cool, but I just *couldn't*, Sarah. Then he showed up here at my place. The next thing I knew we were kissing, and then everything escalated out of control so fast."

My head spun as I remembered the fear on Christian's face when I'd asked him what it was he wanted, the way he'd stepped back to put distance between us because he no longer wanted to be in my space.

Because he didn't *know*.

Who would have thought that word could be sharper than a knife?

"I don't know how I was strong enough to stop, but I was. *Those words* came so close to leaving my mouth."

The pain amplified, squeezing my chest as the word spun around me.

Love. Love. Love.

"I think he knew it . . . somehow saw it in me."

"And what does he feel?"

"I don't think he knows beyond the fact that he wants to have sex with me. He made that much clear." Anger slipped into my voice. I couldn't tell if it was directed at Christian or myself. Like I didn't already know that the first time I met him.

"Elizabeth, he's eighteen. Of course, he wants to have sex with you. That doesn't mean he doesn't care about you."

"But that's the thing, Sarah, I tried to force it out of him, to make him tell me what he feels. He said he didn't know."

I blew out a strained breath. "He said he was sorry then left. And that was it. He keeps calling and saying he's sorry about what happened last night, asking if we can just go back to the way we were before. He has to know that's not going to happen."

It would be impossible.

There's no way I could ever look at him without remembering the way his mouth felt on mine. The way my body had lit on fire.

"I'm sorry, Liz. But you are both so young."

I grunted.

This coming from my sister who'd been with the guy she ended up marrying since she was seventeen. I knew she was just being rational, that we *were* young.

It was true.

But she knew me better than that.

Age had nothing to do with it, although I could only assume it did for Christian. Selfishness like that wasn't easily shed, maturity hard to come by when everything had always been placed at his feet.

"Do you think I wanted to fall in love with him?"

Sarah's voice was soft. "No, and I wasn't minimizing what you feel, Liz. You just worked so hard to make it to New York, and I hate to see you waste it being hung up on a guy like that. He's obviously kind of a jerk."

I sighed and rolled to my back, staring at the ceiling. I'd calmed, the fog in my mind cleared.

Talking with my sister, getting it out, had worked as some kind of soothing balm. "I'm not even mad at him. I'm just mad at myself. It's my fault for trying to make him into something he's not."

The hardest part was I saw the kind of man who could love me buried inside him, waiting to be discovered.

For a fleeting moment last night, I'd seen it staring back at me.

I sensed her shaking her head. "You're kind of amazing, Liz." Her words were filled with sincerity and comfort. "Most girls would be putting all the blame on the guy."

"I am kind of amazing, right?" I forced the tease.

"Now, don't get carried away," she said through a laugh.

I sighed. "Thanks for listening, Sarah. I'm sorry I made this about me. I really am so very happy for you and Greg. I can't wait to be an aunt."

"Hey, I'm here for you whenever you need me. I know it has to be hard for you over there by yourself. And it's Thanksgiving next week. It sucks you're going to miss it. You're still coming home for Christmas, aren't you?"

I couldn't afford to make the trip back twice, and there was no way I'd miss Christmas. "Yeah, I'm coming home."

"Okay, good. Hang in there, Liz. It'll all work out the way it's supposed to."

I had to believe that. "Thanks, Sarah."

"Love you."

"Love you, too."

When I ended the call with my sister, I felt a little better.

Settled.

Resolved.

It was easy to admit it now, what I'd been feeling the last couple of months. The way my stomach would twist when I looked at Christian, the way it hurt when he was away, and how much I couldn't wait until I saw him again.

It was patent in the devastation I'd felt seeing him with another girl last night at the party. Palpable in the way I'd succumbed to his touch when he kissed me.

I was in love with Christian.

Completely.

There was nothing I could do about it. No way to take it back. It was there. Strong. Interwoven and beating with my heart.

I had to end this. The only thing I could do was guard the last part of myself I had, because it would be so easy for me to give it to him now.

Last night, I'd come so close. I would have laid everything else aside while I let him consume me. Let him take it all.

He'd use me. Destroy me. Not because he wanted to, but just because that's who he was.

Flopping onto my stomach, I buried my face in my pillow as if it could block out the depression this realization caused. Last night had cost me my best friend.

But I had to be wise enough to know he wasn't just my friend. He never had been. *This* had always been there, lying in wait, an ambush set to take us over. Being around him was no longer an option.

My heart broke for myself because I'd fallen for someone like him. It broke for Christian because I knew there was a huge part of him who was truly kind.

The part of him who really needed a friend.

But I couldn't be her anymore.

eight

CHRISTIAN

I lay alone in my bed while morning threatened at my window.

Four days had passed since I talked to her.

Each one seemed to add a new element to the sadness that had taken me over.

I was miserable.

There was no other way to describe it.

Empty, vacant, that void I'd tried to fill with Elizabeth's body now a hollow pang.

It was as if Elizabeth had punched me deep in the recesses of my chest, her hands as frantic as mine had been as she searched and struggled.

Ultimately, when she found nothing that I could give her except disappointment, she'd ripped her life from me and left this gaping hole.

And I was the one who'd challenged her to do it.

I tugged my pillow over my face as if it could block out everything I didn't want to see.

"Fuck," I groaned. I tore it from my face and tossed it to the floor. There was nothing that could cover it up or blot it out.

In the cloudy dimness of the room, I sat up and rubbed the pain pressing at my bare chest.

I knew this would happen. I'd take the one pure thing in my life crush it.

The expression Elizabeth had borne Friday night flooded my mind.

In a futile defense, I squeezed my eyes closed against the memory, against the truth of it, but there was nothing I could do to elude it.

The image was like a parasite that had glommed on, dug in, feasting on the ignorance of its host.

It was slowly killing me.

It didn't take long for me to realize something inside me had shattered when I shattered her.

Fear wasn't an emotion I knew well, but I'd never felt it stronger than in that moment when Elizabeth had backed me into a corner with that expression on her face.

Floundering, my body had sought retreat as

she'd silently begged, and I was hit with a fear that had nailed me to her door—fear that she had the capacity to look at me that way, fear that I wanted to touch her so badly, fear that she'd never let me again.

Fear screaming at me to run.

I'd given into the last.

I'd shut her out because I didn't have the strength to handle what was happening between us. I was *eighteen*. I didn't want this. Wasn't ready for it.

But now . . . I raised my face and released a remorseful breath into the stuffy apartment air.

I missed her.

Nothing else seemed to matter but that single truth.

She held so much control over me, and I never even realized it. I mean, yeah, she was my best friend, but losing her shouldn't have hurt this much.

Saturday morning, I left a bunch of messages, trying to make amends, hoping to convince her we could somehow go back to the way we'd been. But each time, I was forced to listen to the sweetness of her voice through her recorded message.

That afternoon, she'd finally called me back. Relief tore through me like a welcomed tempest when my phone had lit up with her number, until her tone seeped through the line, despondent and withdrawn.

"I can't see you anymore, Christian," she'd said through a barely audible whisper. I'd opened my mouth to argue, to convince her that night was just a mistake, to promise I'd find some way to make it right.

Her voice had cracked, and she'd cut me off with a quiet, "Please. I need you to do this for me."

Yeah, I was a fool, but I wasn't stupid.

Even if I tried to convince her otherwise, we both knew that night wasn't a simple misstep. We weren't just two friends messing around, hands and tongue and skin that never should have been. Because I'd never felt anything close to what I'd felt when I kissed her.

She'd hung up the phone without a parting word.

Out of respect, I left her alone. Because I did care about her, even if I was too much a coward to tell her.

The last thing I wanted was to harm her more than I already had, and Elizabeth wanted more from me than I knew how to give.

The night I left, I shut the door between us with a deafening click, but I hadn't gone far. From the other side of her door, I stopped to listen to her weep, felt the magnitude of what I'd done to her.

After that, how could I argue with her when she asked me to leave her alone?

The only hint of her over the last four days had been the back of her head from where she sat far down and across from me in the lecture hall in our American Government class.

The entire class had been spent with me staring down at her, desperate for her to acknowledge me, though she never did. Her hair was piled in a sloppy bun on top of her head, the blonde in complete disarray. In the few fleeting glimpses I'd managed to catch of the side of her face, she'd appeared to be as much of a mess as I was.

That's what this was . . .

A fucking unbearable mess.

When did she become everything without me knowing it?

And was it real or some skewed perception induced by the loss of her presence?

The alarm blared from my nightstand. I reached over and slammed my fist down to silence the shrill sound. Sleep had been scarce, an unfamiliar agitation rising up in my nerves, memories of Elizabeth bleeding together morning and night.

Rolling from bed, I stood and stretched my arms overhead. Everything was sore, inside and out.

Wrong.

Because Elizabeth was gone.

I plodded to the bathroom and switched on the light. The mirror reflected everything I felt.

Sighing, I ran my hand down my cheeks and under my chin. Dark hair shadowed my face because apathy had rid me of the energy to shave since Friday, and my hair was sticking up in every direction.

But it was my eyes that scared me.

They were so . . . lost.

Shit.

With both hands, I held myself up on the sink, dropped my head, and tried to pull it together. Still, I couldn't find anything inside myself that mattered anymore.

I forced myself into the shower and went through the routine. In my dim room, I tossed my dampened towel to the bed and dressed in the quiet.

I just wanted to fix this. To take it back.

But I didn't know how when the memory of how she'd fit so perfectly in my arms reigned supreme.

I'd been seared by her kiss.

Marked by her hands.

My best friend.

I shook my head and slung my backpack onto my shoulders, willing myself into the right frame of mind for my last day of classes before the short Thanksgiving break.

How the hell would I survive through dinner with my parents tomorrow?

Locking my apartment door behind me, I made my way downstairs. I sucked in a sharp breath when a shock of cold air blasted my face.

I headed toward campus, my face down as I forced myself to move. My hands sought warmth in my jeans pockets, my shoulders rigid as I joined the flock of students heading to morning classes.

Sounds filtered in all around me, but none were really heard. I trudged forward, the loss of Elizabeth a thousand pounds added to my feet.

All I wanted to do was turn around, crawl back in bed, and sleep the day away.

Outside my class, students filed inside. I stopped and stared in indecision at the dark hole they disappeared into. People jostled past me, grunted their annoyance as I stood stock still in the middle of the steps.

I couldn't make myself go inside.

Blindly, I wandered the campus, not surprised I ended up in front of the building where Elizabeth's math class was held.

How many times had I sat with her on those steps while she crammed for an extra couple seconds, hurried to ask me a few more questions, stressed that she was going to fail her exam while I promised her she would to do great?

Right now, she'd be inside, sitting at her desk. I could see her there, her head tilted to the side, doodling at the corner of her notebook the way she always did, lost in thought.

Was she thinking of me?

I raked a hand through my hair. Visible breaths filled the ice-cold air as I huffed and began to pace.

What the fuck was I doing?

She'd asked me to leave her alone, and now I was stalking her outside her class.

But I couldn't leave.

I just wanted . . . something. I'd always wanted *something*. From the moment I saw her, I knew it was different, knew it was *more*.

Hovering in the distance of her building door, I willed myself to get it together and honor Elizabeth's wishes.

Randomly, the double doors would open, a few people casually walking in or out, then every ten minutes or so, droves would come or go as a class began or was released.

An hour later, the doors opened again.

A loud flow of students came down the steps as they left for wherever they were going for the holiday.

And I just stood there. Waiting. Waiting for her.

Her head was down when she surfaced behind the crowd at the door. Her feet appeared as heavy as my heart as she made her way down the steps.

My eyes bore into the top of her head, willing her to look up.

I could see it when she felt me, the way she

slowed and her hand reached for the railing to give her support.

Cautiously, she raised her face to mine. She was halfway down the flight of brick steps when she stopped. She stood twenty feet from me, this wistful expression on her face that knocked the air from my lungs.

She no longer appeared angry or hurt. In its place was the same loneliness I'd been swimming in for days, her playful eyes now somber and unsure. Her hair was still a mess, though now it blew free in the short gusts of wind.

My heart thudded. There was no one in the world that could compare to this girl.

She stood frozen, her knuckles white as she gripped the railing, staring at me as I slowly approached.

I stopped at the bottom of the steps. The difference in height brought us face to face.

"What are you doing here?" she whispered, the sound almost lost in the wind.

Regret knotted inside me when she spoke the same words that had spurred our downfall five nights before.

I repeated mine. "*I don't know*, Elizabeth. I don't know anything, except that I *miss* you."

Elizabeth seemed to search for air, struggled to pull in a breath. "Christian—"

I cut her off. "I don't know how to get past

what happened the other night, but I can't go on pretending that I'm okay without you in my life. I haven't slept in days because all I think about is you. I mean . . ."

My tongue darted out to wet my lips, my eyes frantic as they took in every inch of her face.

Agony, the partner to mine, was written there, clear and concise.

"Look at you, Elizabeth." I took a chance and reached out and touched her face.

A bolt of need struck me deep.

Through an open mouth, I released a tremulous breath and took a step away as I softened my voice. "Don't tell me you don't miss me as much as I miss you."

Close enough to be swallowed by her presence, an apprehensive energy vibrated between us. She fidgeted and fisted the hand at her side.

"I miss you, too . . . so much." The last part rasped from her mouth. "But I don't know how to be around you anymore. Don't you see it, Christian?"

She frowned and her head drifted to one side. "Didn't you feel that when you touched me? Do you think either of us can ignore that anymore? Because I can't."

I rushed a nervous hand over my face, trying to clear my thoughts, to offer her something other than the promise she wanted me to make.

"At least come with me tomorrow night. It's Thanksgiving, and I can't stand the thought of you spending it alone. I know I messed up and the last people you probably want to be around are my parents, but I want you there."

I gripped a handful of hair and let the truth bleed out. "I *need* you there, okay? You're my best friend. I meant that, Elizabeth. Even with everything else, you're still my *best friend*. That's all that matters to me."

Softly, her lids fell closed. I could see her wavering, hesitating over every concealed unknown we both wished we could see. She finally opened her eyes, the smallest movement of her head as she timidly nodded. "Okay."

Okay.

My pounding heart steadied, the torment of the last five days silenced.

Okay.

She blinked a thousand questions, the uncertainty in her frame mimicking everything I felt.

Neither of us knew where we were headed or how we'd handle these unanswered questions. The only thing I could do was hang onto her *okay*.

Somehow, I knew we would be.

"We're supposed to meet my parents at the restaurant at 6:00, so I'll meet you at your apartment at 5:30. We'll have to take a cab."

"I'm guessing I need to dress up?"

I offered a compensating laugh and scratched at the nape of my neck. "Uh . . . yeah."

Elizabeth frowned in the cutest way. "Of course, you'd have to make me dress up." That tease was inflected in her tone, the casual ease I loved about Elizabeth.

Maybe we could make it back to that place.

Cocking my chin up and to the side, a playful grin spread my lips. "Oh, you can blame that all on my parents. And I probably don't need to warn you about them. Just plan on a dinner filled with awkward silences interjected with the occasional bouts of my dad criticizing me for being a total failure. Don't worry. Chances are, they won't find you worth looking twice in your direction."

I injected as much humor as I could dish into the words, though they still came with a bite.

An early apology for what I was about to put her through.

I felt obligated to warn her how absolutely terrible dinner would be. How callus my parents truly were. Honestly, I hated to subject her to them, but I wasn't lying when I told her I needed her there.

That tenderness I could never deserve surfaced on her face again, a sympathy only offered in the kindness of my friend.

"I get it, Christian." Her arm swung out, her

fingers grazing just the side of my hand. "I'm going for you. Not for them."

I tensed my shoulders and rocked up onto my toes, then back onto my heels. "I promise I'll take you out for ice cream afterward to make up for it."

One side of her mouth lifted, and a small laugh fluttered from her perfect mouth. "It's a deal."

I struggled with the urge to kiss her, tried to remember the lines that had been drawn that now were blurred and smeared, tried to trace back to that moment months before when I'd come to the resolution of who we were and what she meant to me.

I stepped back, minutely shaking my head, realizing Elizabeth could never be contained by that definition.

"I'll see you tomorrow," I whispered.

"I'll be ready."

Elizabeth brushed past me and ambled down the corridor with her head held low again.

I watched her go.

When she glanced at me over her shoulder, my chest tightened. The movement was pensive, searching.

A small, thankful smile tugged at one side of my mouth, and my hand fluttered up in a hesitant wave.

She smiled back. And I saw it again, the way she looked at me that night.

It singed my skin, warmed my face, expanded and pushed at my ribs.

I rubbed at my chest, shaken by the impact of her parting glance.

Pushing it off, I instead savored the respite I found in her *okay*.

When she disappeared into the milling crowd, I turned around and ran to catch the last couple minutes of my class.

I took my time getting ready for Thanksgiving dinner. It's not like I could sit around alone in my apartment any longer. All I wanted was to be back in Elizabeth's presence, to see her face and again be reminded that we would be *okay*.

I dressed in black dress pants, a dark maroon button-up, and a matching tie, then ran some product through my hair to maintain some semblance of style.

The last thing I needed was to give my father another reason to tear into me.

I'd called my mom yesterday to tell her to make reservations for four because I was bringing a friend.

She'd hesitated, before she scolded me for doing something like this when I knew it would upset my father.

I flat out told her I didn't give a shit what my

father thought. They were the last two people I wanted to spend Thanksgiving with, anyway.

How sad was that?

I dreaded seeing them.

My own parents.

Sometimes I thought maybe my mother tried, but most of the time, she was like some mindless robot next to my father, as if she didn't have her own feelings or something.

The only thing that would make it halfway bearable was Elizabeth being there.

I glanced at the clock as I tied my too-shiny black shoes, anxious to get to her. I knew Elizabeth was stepping out, throwing herself into a world where she would feel completely uncomfortable, and I knew she was only doing it for me.

Selfless.

Exactly the opposite of me.

This girl was like none other.

At 5:15, I pulled on my jacket and left my apartment. It was freezing outside. I paused to look up.

Heavy, dark clouds hung low, the tops of the skyscrapers disappearing into the winter sky. Night pressed in, and a chill rolled down my spine.

I blew into my hands and rubbed them together before I buried them deep in my coat pockets for warmth. Turning, I headed in Elizabeth's direction.

Outside her building, I looked up to the second floor where her light glowed from behind her drapes. Blood rushed to my ears, and my pulse bolted ahead of me.

Get it together.

Drawing in a steadying breath, I bounded up the steps. My hand shook when I lifted it to her door. I rapped at the wood.

"One second," echoed from the other side.

Impatience shuffled my feet, and I jerked my head up when the door suddenly flew open.

Warmth blasted across my face, and Elizabeth stood there, framed in her doorway.

For a flash, we both froze.

Trapped.

Contemplating the other.

I smiled lightly as my gaze traveled her face, making sure she was there, that she wanted to be beside me as much as I wanted to be beside her.

Tonight, she wore more makeup than I'd ever seen her wear, her brown eyes kissed with gold and browns and shimmer, rimmed in black. Her hair was twisted up with pieces tumbling down in all the right places.

Every time she blinked, I was struck, mesmerized, the perfection of this girl something that had undone me.

My gaze traveled down.

There were a rare few in this world who could

stop me in my tracks, but it was only Elizabeth who could bring me to my knees. Her white collared blouse was fitted, the buttons starting just at the top of the cleft of her breasts. Her black skirt was flowy and swished just above her knees. She wore nylons and heels, something I'd never witnessed her in before.

My mouth was dry by the time I looked back at her face, and her cheeks had reddened with my obvious perusal.

I cleared my throat, my voice low. "You look amazing, Elizabeth."

Stunning. Breathtaking.

One of her hands fluttered up to her neck, and she self-consciously toyed with a piece of hair that had fallen from the twist. "Thank you."

Finally, unease seemed to cause her to tear herself away. She turned her back to me, leaving the door open.

"Come on in. Let me grab my purse and coat."

The words rushed from her mouth in a tumble, an awkwardness rising in the air, tension that neither of us knew how to deal with. The click of her heels on her hardwood floor punctuated the nerves firing between us.

And I should have known it would be this way, that like Elizabeth had said, whatever this was could no longer be ignored.

The second I stepped through her apartment

door, it all crashed over me—the way she had smelled, the way she had tasted, the way she had felt.

My body reacted, and I was picturing her up against the counter, could hear the sounds that had whispered from her mouth.

I squeezed my eyes and attempted to will it away. Maybe Elizabeth was right. Maybe I couldn't be around her, because I could do nothing to control the desire from belting me now.

When she looked back at me, I knew she felt it, too.

Regret twitched her face as her eyes flitted to the same spot where my mind had just been, but then she turned away and pulled on a long, heavy gray coat.

She grabbed a small purse she clutched in her hand. "Are you ready to go?"

Forcing the reaction down, I smiled, and this time I made it a promise. I would do anything to ensure we were okay. "Yup. Let's get out of here."

I swung the door open and stood aside so she could go ahead of me before I followed her out the door. I jiggled her knob to be sure it was locked.

Our footsteps echoed as we carefully made our way down the stairwell. Elizabeth walked slower than normal, traversing the stairs in heels, her breaths short and rasped and filling up the enclosed space.

"Are you nervous?" I asked.

Slowing, she glanced over her shoulder, that same expression on her face. "Yes."

My feet couldn't move when she looked at me that way, and I gripped the railing and sucked in a breath when that feeling struck me again.

Elizabeth continued on, and cold air gusted into the stairwell when Elizabeth opened the door.

Ahead of me, she held open the door, fighting a shudder and dipping her head in an attempt to protect herself from the surge of winter blanketing the city that blasted into the stairwell.

Fumbling to a stop, she pressed her hand over her mouth to stifle a gasp.

"Oh my God," she whispered. She pushed the door wide and rushed out into the night.

What was she doing?

The door swung closed behind her, and I found my footing and ran down the last few steps to follow her out.

I froze just outside the door.

Elizabeth was there, in the middle of the sidewalk, her arms and face raised to the sky as she slowly spun in a circle.

I stuffed my hands in my pockets to block out some of the chill and stood there watching as little flecks of snow flitted down and melted on the soft skin of Elizabeth's face.

It was one of the most meager shows of

snowfall I'd ever seen, but to Elizabeth, it appeared to be the most magical thing she'd ever witnessed.

The smile on her face was enough to light up the whole town.

Enough to light up my life.

She spun around, looked back at me as if I hadn't been the culprit of our downfall five days earlier.

Flashes of joy sparked in her eyes. "Christian . . . can you believe it? It's snowing."

She shook her head in awe and lifted her face back to the lights reflected in the stormy night sky.

Wrapped up in this momentous event, Elizabeth seemed to be more thankful than I had the capacity to make sense of because it was something I'd taken for granted my entire life.

Beauty.

It slammed into me so hard it nearly knocked me from my feet. At the same time, it felt completely natural.

Inevitable.

Simple.

I loved her.

My eyes dropped closed, savoring the truth soaking my body, my nerves thrilling in excitement while my heart beat with a steady content.

I loved her.

I opened my eyes to find her staring over at me, her arms held up just at her sides, as if she'd caught sight of me and had been trapped in that very spot. "What's wrong?"

A breath escaped through my nose, manifested in the cold air, the space between us too great. "Nothing's wrong, Elizabeth. Everything is perfect."

Her nose curled up a little, and her head barely tipped to the side. I thought maybe she didn't quite believe me and was searching for something.

A question piqued her gentle smile, before she turned her attention back to the fleeting white dotting the sky.

I wondered if she could she see it in me the same way I'd seen it in her. If she knew in that moment she'd unlocked something in me, and I'd never be the same.

She stole one last glance at the fluttering sky. "We'd better grab a cab or we're going to be late."

I shook myself off. "Yeah. You ready for this?"

Light laughter tipped from Elizabeth's mouth, the sound echoing in the stiff winter air. "No, not at all."

I came in close to her side, smiled down at the girl I loved. "Me neither."

nine

The hushed winter pressed down from above.

Flurries danced as they fell.

Expanding my lungs with a breath of freezing cold air, I struggled to quell the hammer knocking against my ribs, sought the peace found in the beauty of this night sky.

Christian's fingers brushed down the inside of my arm before he wound them at the crook of my elbow. His fingertips pulsed twice at the sensitive spot, as if tapping out a message, before they settled and found a secure hold burrowed in my skin.

A flit of uncontained nerves rose as goose bumps along my flesh, and I bit at my lip to cover my reaction.

I didn't know if I could ever feel better than I did right then.

A sense of awe sank down deep into my bones, softening the reservations I had about agreeing to attend this dinner with Christian.

Never before had I seen snow. The spots where it had fallen and melted against my skin still stung and burned, but the memory covered me like an embrace.

But it was Christian's touch that had my head spinning.

I guessed when I'd agreed to this dinner, I thought we'd fight to get back to the place where we were just friends. I thought we'd shove our feelings down like we'd been doing for so long, and that those feelings would fester and grow until we found ourselves in a situation so much like the one we'd been in last Friday night.

I peeked up at him just as he looked down to catch my wondering gaze.

One side of his mouth lifted, his eyes soft as they traced my face, and he squeezed my arm a little tighter.

Going back didn't seem to be a part of Christian's intentions.

Something had changed from the moment

Christian had shown up at my apartment door until he held onto me now, as if the beauty falling around us had the power to chase away all our unanswered questions.

He leaned in close to my face, his head tilted to the side. "I'm so glad you're coming."

He'd broken me down so easily.

Relief had come like the blaring horn of a freight train when I'd seen him standing outside my class, his beautiful face marred with the same affliction I'd drowned in for the last week.

I'd tried to resist him, to tell him why I had to be true to the decision I'd made.

But in the end, I'd missed him too much. The hole he left behind was too great. There was nothing I could do but concede.

Being around him had become a risk I was willing to take.

"I'm glad I am, too."

He pulled back a bit, and his smile widened before he turned to raise his free hand to hail an approaching cab.

Our breaths rose up and mixed in the crisp night air. The fingers loosened at my arm and glided down to take my hand as the cab pulled to the curb. Christian opened the door and stood aside.

"Scoot in first." He pressed his palm lightly to the small of my back.

Energy sparked with the light contact. My heart leapt to my throat.

Being around Christian had thrown my nerves into overdrive.

I scooted all the way across the back seat. Adjusting my skirt, I pulled the seat belt across my chest and snapped it in place.

Christian plopped down beside me with a heavy exhale. "I can't believe how cold it is out there."

He puffed hot air from his lungs into the cup of his hands before he rubbed them together, then turned his face my direction.

Dim light from the streetlamps bled through the windows, illuminating the confined space. Chunks of black hair had come loose from the style he'd tried to tame it into, pieces sticking up in every direction they shouldn't be.

His chin was held strong in an emotion I didn't understand, his mouth twisted in a timid smile.

But his eyes . . . Was I wrong, what I saw there? The same thing I thought I'd glimpsed on the sidewalk when we left my apartment five minutes earlier?

I got lost there, in the expression of his face that conveyed everything I wanted him to feel.

Internally, I cautioned myself.

Images from last weekend sped in blips across my vision.

I thought of how I'd begged him with my body

before I'd begged him with my mouth to feel the same way I did, and I was haunted by his expression when he'd walked out my door.

I had to remember the devastation that had made it hard to get out of bed in the days he'd been gone.

The truth was, I was so desperate for him that I would delude myself into believing this was something it was not. The cliff was so close, my knees weak and my feet fumbling as I struggled to balance, my heart on the line. I was one slip from complete destruction. Christian would own me with a flick of his fingers.

He leaned forward and grasped the headrest in his hands, giving the driver directions to the restaurant. His long body filled the small space, his knees pressed up against the back of the seat.

The driver nodded, and Christian sat back and adjusted himself into a comfortable position, pulling the seatbelt across his chest.

The car merged into traffic, the silence thick as the simmering darkness within the cab surrounded us.

I stole a glance to my left. Well, it wasn't exactly stolen since Christian was already looking at me.

He rested one side against the door, his elbow on the windowsill and his head propped in his hand as he unabashedly stared. Streetlamps flashed through the windows in quick succession as the cab traveled down the road, illuminating flickers of the stark intensity of his blue eyes.

Heat rose to my cheeks and a gradual tingle diffused across my skin. If I could have, I would have turned away, but I was trapped, locked in whatever was happening deep in the recesses of Christian's mind.

It was smothering, surged out in waves, a tide that seemed to break against us both.

I squirmed in my seat, and Christian wet his lips, the lump in his throat bobbing as he swallowed.

"Are you missing your mom today?"

His question jarred me from the turmoil tumbling through my mind, reminding me that, no matter what, Christian was my best friend. He cared about me.

"Yeah." Although really, half the day had been spent worrying that I'd made a mistake when I gave in to him yesterday. Of course, the other half had been watching the clock because I couldn't wait to see him again.

I cleared the surprise from my throat. "I talked to my mom earlier. My older sister, Sarah, and her husband are going over to my mom's, and of course my little sister is there. I didn't get to tell you . . . Sarah is having a baby. I get to be an aunt."

With the thought, a big smile pulled up at one corner of my mouth. I felt bad that I hadn't taken enough time to think of my sister, how amazing her news was, that she was bringing a child into this world.

I couldn't wait to see that baby's precious face.

Christian's face murmured a smile. "Yeah? That's awesome, Elizabeth. I bet you wish you were there right now."

My shoulders rose in an uncertain shrug. Did I? I knew I should. But right then, I felt like this was exactly where I was supposed to be.

One side of his mouth quivered. "Does it make me selfish that what I'm giving thanks for today is you being here with me?" He shifted and fidgeted with a button on his coat. "I don't know where I'd be right now if it hadn't been you in that café at the beginning of the year."

"Christian." Unrecognizable questions wove into my tone, so much contained in just his name.

My pulse spiked when Christian slid his hand slowly across the seat, the movement calculated. His chin tipped to the side and he flipped his hand so his palm was up. This time, he didn't just take my hand or guide me into what he wanted.

He waited.

It was an invitation, one subject to a decision from me.

My eyes flicked from his hand to his face. I wavered, a gush of air suffusing into the cab as I deliberated.

I wanted to ask him, *what does this mean?*

I wanted reassurance. For him to ease the ache that had bound itself to the beat of my heart, for him to say he wanted me in the same way I wanted him, and that I wasn't making the biggest mistake of my young life.

Instead, I wove my fingers through his.

As if he found as much relief in the contact as I did, a sigh fluttered from Christian's mouth, and he squeezed my hand.

"I'm so glad you're here," he said again, shaking me up more.

The cab came to a stop, bringing an end to whatever Christian and I had just shared.

Even if that was it, if we shared nothing more, I'd cherish it, because I would swear, for a few seconds, Christian knew he felt *more*, even if he didn't know how to admit it.

Venting a sound of frustration, Christian wrenched a hand through his hair when the valet opened my door. He seemed as opposed to leaving the safety of the cab as I was.

"Looks like we're here," he said, stating the obvious as he pulled his hand from mine.

Inclining his head for me to go on, I accepted the help of the doorman and stood from the cab. For a moment, I was alone, fidgeting as a new dread came to settle in the pit of my stomach.

My nerves rocketed as I absorbed my surroundings. Christian was right. The last people I wanted to spend Thanksgiving with were his parents, and the last place I wanted to spend it was somewhere like this. No question the building was beautiful, but pretention poured from its walls, an excessive display of glass and marble and brass.

What the hell was I doing here? I normally wasn't one of those girls who felt ill at ease in their own skin. I liked who I was. But here, I had no place.

Christian sidled up to me. Like it belonged there, his hand went straight to the small of my back. "Let's get you out of the cold," he encouraged, turning us up the runner.

The attendant opened the door and stood aside with a clipped nod of his head.

I lifted my gaze to Christian to find a slight grimace when he turned his chin down to me, an apology, as if he knew how nervous this all made me. I didn't even know what *we* were anymore, and now I had to face his parents with all those dizzying questions mucking up my mind.

We checked our coats, and Christian led us to the podium where the maître de stood. "Reservation for Richard Davison."

The man scanned his book. "The rest of your party has already arrived. Right this way."

Subdued conversations created a dull hum in the overly elegant space. Waiters in tuxes balanced silver trays, flitting silently around the room. Light clatters of silverware seemed the most distinct sound.

I tensed amidst it all.

No.

Definitely not a place I wanted to spend Thanksgiving. It wasn't as if I'd never been to a nice restaurant before, but this place was over the top.

Christian leaned in close to my shoulder and mumbled, "I told you this would be miserable."

I faked a smile. "It's fine. It'll be great."

He laughed under his breath. "You're the worst liar I've ever met."

His hand dropped from my back and found my hand, weaving our fingers together. Part of me wanted to jerk away, to stop the flow of confusion I felt from the overt gesture, to hide whatever *this* was from his parents, to cut off the longing it ignited within me, but I couldn't let go.

Christian's hand constricted on mine when the maître de stopped in front of his parents' table.

The man dipped his head. "Your party."

Christian said, "Thank you," but I found I could give no response as I fixated on the couple in front of me.

Oh God. What had Christian dragged me into?

Two of the most beautiful people I'd ever seen sat looking up at us. My gaze waffled between the two of them, shocked by the striking resemblance

Christian bore to his mother and stricken by the coldness in his father.

There was something about his hard stare that made it difficult to look away, although the man's contemplation easily jumped between Christian and me.

There was little semblance between father and son other than the thatch of black hair perfectly tailored on Mr. Davison's head.

His mother was waif thin and wore a silk two-piece skirt suit. Jewels dripped from every exposed surface of her body. I could only guess the long hair she had in a stylish coif had been dyed blonde, and she wore her chin permanently lifted in an elevated air of self-righteousness.

Unease had me shifting my feet as I shrank back from the severity of their presence.

"Mom, Dad, this is my friend, Elizabeth Ayers. Elizabeth, this is my father, Richard Davison, and my mother, Claire Davison."

Christian released the death grip he had on me and gestured in my direction, although thankfully, he chose not to move far from my side.

Richard Davison slowly rose from his seat and extended a brusque hand across the table. "So nice to meet you, Elizabeth."

Wrapping his hand around mine, Christian's father shook my hand. It was firm, hard, unwelcoming.

There was nothing nice about it.

"Nice to meet you, Mr. Davison," I forced around the lump in my throat.

When I turned and accepted Christian's mother's hand, it was cool to the touch, clammy. "Very nice to meet you, Elizabeth." It was all form and pomp, insincere.

I struggled to keep my hand from trembling in hers and searched for confidence, reminding myself I was doing this for Christian. "Very nice to meet you, too, Mrs. Davison. Thank you for having me."

In return, she offered a tight nod of her head and folded herself back under the table.

Christian pulled the chair out for me and helped me settle. Almost inconspicuously, he brushed his fingers under my elbow, a silent buoy to my spirit. I would suffer through this for him.

"Thank you," I murmured under my breath as I adjusted in my seat. We were handed our menus, and I crossed my feet at my ankles as I sat up straight in the chair. Rigid. Impressing people had never been something I was interested in, but something about these two told me I would fare better pretending to fit into a place where I so obviously did not.

This was going to be a long night.

I glanced above my menu to find Christian's father watching me with the concentration of a hawk about to swoop in on its prey.

My attention dropped back to the words, but I could still feel his eyes penetrating through the thickness of parchment and leather.

In silence, we studied the menus. When the waiter arrived, I ordered a water and the Thanksgiving special, hoping to make the least impact with my presence as possible.

After our orders were taken, Christian's father sat back in his seat, still studying me. "So, Elizabeth, how did you and Christian meet?"

I swallowed and swiped my napkin across my mouth. I stole a glance at Christian, and he just smiled at me in encouragement. I turned my attention back to his father. "We both signed up to be paired with a study partner in our American Government class, and Christian turned out to be mine."

Richard Davison nodded, and I thought maybe it was an acceptable answer.

I sucked in a little breath of relief. Maybe I could handle this.

"And where are you from?"

"San Diego."

"A long way from home." It wasn't a question, just an observation I was sure was tied to another thought.

"Yes," I said.

"So why New York?"

"I've always dreamed of moving here. Columbia University was my first choice."

"Hmm. It's a hard school to get into." Another observation.

"Yes," I agreed.

God, I wasn't prepared for this, to be set on display, subject to Richard Davison's scrutiny. I'd counted on Christian's promise that his parents would find me so inconsequential that they wouldn't look twice in my direction.

Mr. Davison sat back while his salad plate was removed and a soup bowl was set in its place. "And what do your parents do?"

My nerves flared, and I shifted uncomfortably in my seat. I'd always been proud of my family, but everything about his demeanor put me on the defensive. "Um . . . just my mom. My dad left when I was young, and my mother has always worked in manufacturing."

He lifted his brow. "Design?"

I minimally shook my head. "No. She works on the floor."

Whatever interest Richard Davison had in me was silenced in my response, as if my answer had given him all the information he needed.

I was sure I could hear the silent judgement rippling from him.

That I was below them. Not good enough to be sitting beside their son.

Tension fell over the table, and Christian brushed his fingers down my leg, another apology, one I couldn't even acknowledge.

Instead I stared at his father, contending with the powerful urge I had to defend my mother, to tell him how hard she worked to feed us and keep a decent roof over our heads.

I remained silent because it was clear in Richard Davison's eyes nothing I said would matter, anyway.

My assumptions made about Christian's parents were right. They were as hollow as I suspected, bred too high, their heads filled with too much.

Christian had never had a chance.

Is this what he would become? Would he succumb to the mold of his father?

To the distance in his mother?

Be shaped into this machine that cared for nothing?

The thought soured and caused nausea to roll in my stomach. God. I couldn't stand the thought of this happening to him, for the light in his eyes to dim and the playfulness in his smile to fade.

Finally, the main course was served.

Christian's mother sipped at her wine, and in between bites filled Christian in on the elite. "Did you hear Stephen Bell and Emily Cann are engaged?" She tittered a laugh. "Who would have thought those two families would come together?

That will be quite the fortune for their children. Oh, and the Graham's have sold their house and bought a historical downtown . . ."

I had to squash the urge to roll my eyes. Christian's mother hadn't seen him in months, and this was all she could offer him? Gossip? She never even asked him how he was, if he was happy or troubled or was struggling in any way.

Longing inflamed my already homesick heart. The idea that I didn't want to be home for Thanksgiving all but evaporated.

What I would give to be in the midst of the shuffle of my mother's kitchen now, the scents rising up from the oven as the turkey cooked to perfection. What I would give to feel the tender hand of my mother while she pushed my hair back from my face as I peeled potatoes, how she'd be so thankful that all of her daughters were there.

The only difference was I wanted Christian there with me.

I peeked over at him. He ate in outright discomfort, though with an obvious sense of normalcy.

A pang struck me at my core.

He'd never had that—love without expectations, someone there to cherish him despite his faults, someone to praise him for his strengths.

The love I'd been too scared to acknowledge before glowed and burned, whipped and stirred as it grew. From the outside, it was nearly impossible to see the damage his parents had created on the inside of that gorgeous exterior.

As he sat there now, it was obvious, these bold marks of ruin that scored his spirit.

Casting a furtive glance in his parents' direction, I cut another piece of turkey and brought it to my mouth. Could they really not see him the way I did?

"So, Christian, tell me how your classes are going," his father said between bites.

Christian stiffened.

Here we go.

I wondered how his father had restrained himself this long.

Clearing his throat before he spoke, Christian seemed to measure his words to evoke the least reaction from his father. "They're going really, really well. My grades are good. Just have to make it through finals and I should have all As."

"Mmm . . ." his father mused, sliding a forkful of mashed potatoes into his arrogant mouth. "You know you need to focus these next couple of weeks. Don't for a minute get confident. It just takes one slip and you'll lose all the footing you have."

"I know that, Dad. We study constantly."

It was clear in the way Christian's eyes darted in my direction that his assertion included me.

We.

Richard Davison's brow arched in speculation, his appraisal clear and unjust. "And you think it's wise to distract yourself this way?" he asked Christian, though his gaze remained unwavering, locked on me in decided disgust.

The man had no right to look at me like that.

I struggled to maintain a straight face, reminded myself I was here because I'd been invited, remembered my mom had always taught me to be respectful, even when someone so obviously didn't deserve it.

"Dad, you have no idea how much Elizabeth has helped me this semester. She studies just as hard, if not harder, than I do. She's going to be an attorney, too."

I could feel Christian almost pleading with his father to like me, the way his body drifted forward and his head tipped to the side in supplication.

A condescending smile cracked Richard Davison's face. "Oh, really? Don't you two make the perfect little couple."

"Dad," Christian begged beneath his breath, his body jerking in embarrassment.

"We're just friends." The sudden denial flew from my mouth. Saying it felt like a lie.

Christian blanched, and the dislike on his father's face grew. Neither of them believed it either.

I blinked hard, as if I could deflect whatever blow was coming. I could feel it, this quiet hostility that had built throughout the night, this agitation that had his father sitting on edge.

Richard Davison leaned in across the table with his voice quieted. "Do you even understand the amount of work this is going to take, Christian? The devotion required if you plan to take over for me one day?"

"Of course, I do."

"Do you? Really? Do you have any idea the foundation I've set to ensure my son has the best opportunities? The best chance at succeeding in life?"

"God, Dad, would you just lay off me for once? I get it. It's fine."

His father's voice dropped lower, though it hardened. "Goddamn it, Christian, it is not fine. Have you not learned one single thing I've tried to teach you? You can't waste this time. It is more important now than ever to stay focused on your goals."

Christian straightened in his chair, his voice just as low and tight as his father's. "Not everything is about what you want."

His father just laughed below his breath, though there was no hint of humor. It was mocking.

"You have no idea what strings I had to pull to get you here, do you?"

My attention darted to Christian to watch his face fall as understanding dawned.

How could his father be so cruel? To do this now, in front of an audience?

I wanted to speak, to touch Christian's arm and tell him that his father was wrong. I'd never met anyone as intelligent as him or who worked as hard.

But I could say nothing before his father spoke again. "You're so ignorant you don't even notice when a gold digger is trying to sink her claws into you."

In shock, I froze, then humiliation unfurled over me in a hot sheet of disgrace. With what he was insinuating, he may as well have slapped me across the face.

I jerked my chin to the side to block the blow, felt tears welling under the surface. I would not let this guy see me cry.

Fumbling out of my chair and onto my feet, I steadied myself on the table as I wobbled on the heels I was so unaccustomed to wearing.

Mortified, Christian looked up at me. He wrapped a gentle hand my wrist. "Elizabeth, please, don't go."

How could he ask me to stay?

I shook my head and twisted from his grasp. "I'm sorry, Christian, but I can't do this."

Sorrow tore me straight through as I finally let

that flicker of hope I'd clung to all night slip away.

I didn't belong in his world, could never fit into it. I was strong enough to know I didn't want to.

I'd never strive for money or position, had no intention of spending my life sitting like some mindless bimbo next to a man just because I wanted something from him. I couldn't stand the thought that Richard Davison had even planted the idea in Christian's mind.

As much as I loved Christian, I refused to subject myself to *this*. I felt violated.

Wronged.

Remorseful blue eyes stared up at me. My heart hurt so much for him. This was his life, the way he'd been raised.

"I'm so sorry, Christian," I said again. This time, my words were a goodbye.

Heat burned my ears and tears stung my eyes as I turned to flee. Wearing my embarrassment like a coat, I twisted through the tables to make an escape. I forced myself forward, praying I'd get outside before the tears began to fall.

I didn't take the time to get my jacket from the front. I fled out the door.

The sharp bite of cold slammed me. I sucked in a ragged breath and pushed myself forward. My heels clattered as I clamored toward the street.

Relief slipped between my lips as a small cry when I saw the two cabs waiting at the curb.

"A cab, please," I nearly begged as I ran, struggling to keep myself upright as I approached the cab.

A hand grabbed my upper arm before I could make it inside. I knew it was him. The hold was firm but gentle, filled with as much confusion as I felt. I needed to get away from him as much as I wanted to stay. I struggled to break free.

He spun me around and cupped my cheeks, forcing me to look at him. "Fuck . . . Elizabeth . . . would you just stop for a second?"

With the sound of his voice, the tears broke free. I tried to hide them, to tug away from the hold Christian had on me, heart and soul.

His tongue darted out to wet his lips, his eyes searching as they took in every emotion firing across my face.

"I can't believe he pulled that shit in front of you." His hold tightened in emphasis. "Tell me you know I would never think that about you. It doesn't matter who I brought, they would never be good enough, Elizabeth. I will never be good enough. Don't you see that?"

Tender fingers came up to brush the hair from my face, to wipe my tears.

"I hate him, Elizabeth . . . hate that he would make you feel this way."

I wrestled to discern what I felt, who I was angry with and who I was running from.

All I came up with was another question, another miserable *why*.

Why did I have to love someone like him so much? The moment he walked through the café door, my instincts had told me to run. Why had I been such a fool to put myself in the position to be standing here now?

But none of this was really Christian's fault. We were separated by a gap neither of us had created, each a product of our heritage, a distant span of cultures that made us completely incompatible.

"Just go back inside with your family, Christian."

Shaking his head, his grip increased, the slight sting of his fingertips digging into my cheeks. "No. It's Thanksgiving and I want to spend it with you."

"They're your *family*, and I don't mean anything to you." My assertion rang with deceit.

"How can you say that? You mean everything to me." Christian pressed his lips to my forehead, this gentle show of affection that weakened my knees and left me gripping his wrists, desperate to believe every one of his words.

And I felt it again, a glimmer of what I'd seen in his eyes earlier.

I longed for it.

His father's mocking voice found us from somewhere behind Christian. "Just friends, huh? Looks that way to me. She's a waste of your time,

Christian. Put her in a cab and come back inside where you belong."

A tortured cry erupted from my throat.

"Just go inside, where you belong," I rasped, mimicking his father's words, tripping over the heartbreak that had lodged in my throat.

"Elizabeth . . ." Christian wavered, looking back to where his father stood confronting us.

The gap.

Christian held no true conviction. He didn't know whether to stand up for me or give in to his father. He still didn't *know*.

I ripped myself from his hold and jumped into the cab. Christian just stood there, staring at me.

My spirit splintered a little more.

I slammed the door shut behind me to shut Christian out. The cab driver looked up in the mirror, and I cried out, "Go . . . please . . . just go."

I slumped back in the seat as the cab jerked into traffic. My head sagged back on the headrest and I lifted my face to the ceiling. Tears streaked down the sides of my face and ran into my hair. Reaching up to scrub them away, I released a bitter bark into the air.

I already knew this. When did I forget?

Christian Davison was so off limits.

ten

Motherfucker.

I wanted to scream.

Instead, I just stood there staring in shock as Elizabeth's cab drove away.

The day I finally got it—accepted it—had to be the same day I laid her at my parents' feet.

Slowly, I turned around to face my father.

He stood near the restaurant door. Smugness clung to his posture, his jaw tight and shoulders squared as he stared me down.

Embarrassment and anger seethed in my veins, curling my hands into fists. So many years I'd strived to be just like him, and now I was ashamed to even know him.

A taunting snort slipped through his nose and he just barely shook his head. It was full of condescension, as if daring me to contend with him. "Come back inside and finish your dinner."

He spun on his heel, like what had just happened mattered none.

"What is wrong with you?" I called out just before he disappeared through the door. "I invited her here and you insult her? She's my *friend*."

Pausing, he craned his neck around to look at me. Then he laughed, this incredulous sound that punched me in the gut. "She's trash, Christian."

The words knocked around in my head.

Elizabeth . . . this girl . . . the one.

The strongest surge of protectiveness welled up inside me, and I took two steps toward him.

"*I love her.*" I felt pride saying it aloud, the kind of pride I'd put money down that my father had never experienced.

His face slowly twisted and he shook his head as if he didn't know me at all. "Then you're more of fool than I pegged you for. Now get inside. Your mother and I flew all the way here to spend Thanksgiving with you. You're ruining our evening."

He shook his arms out and looked down to adjust the cuffs of his sleeves.

For so long, he'd controlled every aspect of my life. My goals, my beliefs, what I wanted, and where I was going. Was I really going to allow him to dictate who I cared about?

"Fuck this," I muttered under my breath.

His head jerked up. "What did you just say?"

"I said, fuck this. I'm out of here."

He clenched his jaw. I could almost hear him grinding his teeth. "Don't you even think about it, Christian."

I scoffed. "What are you going to do, *Dad*," I spat out his name. "Cut me out of your life? Keep me out of the firm?"

I laughed. There was no way. That would be a direct reflection on him, his own failure at conforming me into what he wanted me to be.

Walking backward, I lifted both hands in the air as I retreated. Not in surrender, but in opposition. This was one area of my life I wouldn't allow him to control.

Then I turned around and leapt into the backseat of a waiting cab. Elizabeth's address was already passing through my urgent lips as I slammed the door shut. "Hurry, please."

The driver kind of smiled. He had probably been there to witness what had gone down with Elizabeth a couple minutes earlier. "Sure."

The ride felt like the longest ten minutes of my life.

When he stopped outside her building, Elizabeth was pulling open the door to her building. I threw some money on the front seat. "Thanks, man."

"No problem."

I jumped from the car and back into the winter cold, yelling her name. "Elizabeth!"

Slowly, she spun around, her hand still on the door handle, as if she had every intention of leaving me standing there.

"Christian." Frustration spun through her tone, though I could hear the tears in her words, could see them marking her face. I'd hurt her again. And I hated it.

"Just leave me alone," she said.

But this time, I knew walking out wasn't an option. "I can't."

It was snowing again, harder this time, a steady grazing of white that dusted the city. My heavy breaths turned to vapor as I stood in front of her, panting, trying to gather my thoughts, to rein everything in.

I couldn't.

One side of Elizabeth's mouth trembled, and she looked at me in both wariness and exhaustion. She dropped her hold on the door to completely face me.

"I don't understand what you want from me, Christian. You drag me to this dinner with your parents, and then when your father attacks me, you can't even stand up for me?"

"You didn't give me a chance to."

Wisps of blonde kissed along her jaw, pieces sticking to the contours of her perfect face.

God, she was beautiful.

Love and fear vacillated across her features, uncertainty and want.

Something throbbed inside me, so deep it swallowed me whole.

When Elizabeth had changed me, I didn't know. But she did. She'd unhinged something that had been locked inside, something I'd never believed I wanted or even knew existed. But with her standing there, it was all I could see.

Approaching her slowly, I stopped close and lifted her chin with my finger so she'd look at me.

I searched her face.

Her eyes dropped away, even though I held her firm.

"I'm here now. You think I wouldn't stand up to my father for you? That I'd just stand there and let him talk about you like that? This week has been the worst of my life, Elizabeth, every single minute that you weren't a part of it. And then yesterday when you agreed to go with me tonight, I can't describe the relief I felt."

Her warm brown gaze finally fluttered up to meet with mine. I slid my fingers from her chin and cupped one side of her face. Touching her was perfection.

Exhaling heavily, I inclined my face closer and caressed my thumb over her cheek. "And tonight . . . I can't even begin to apologize for what happened tonight. I can only tell you I don't care what my dad thinks about us."

I brought my other hand to her face and squeezed in emphasis. "Elizabeth, I can't lose you."

She wet her lips and shivered. She hugged herself, her crossed arms a barrier between us. "I don't even know what that means, Christian. One minute, you're telling me you want to get past what happened last Friday so we can be friends again, and the next minute, you're holding my hand and telling me I mean everything to you."

Frantic brown eyes begged as they flitted across my face, as if she were desperate to find an answer there. "I don't understand what you want from me."

Increasing my hold, I edged closer. "I want you. I want you to take a chance on me. I know I haven't given you a reason to, and everything between us is a mess right now, but it's only because we aren't what we're supposed to be. I've been fighting this so hard for so long because I thought I was protecting our friendship when all I was doing was setting us up to fail."

Hot tears fell into my hands, and Elizabeth's mouth dropped open. I resisted the desire to crush her to me, to kiss her, to finally take what I'd always known was supposed to be mine, although in a completely different way than the initial urge that had me squirming in my seat four months prior.

Instead, it galloped ahead of me, a future I'd never believed I wanted. One I knew without a single doubt I wanted to share with Elizabeth.

"Elizabeth, I haven't touched another girl since that first time I walked out of your apartment. I mean, I tried . . . but all I could think about was you. All this time, it was you."

"What?" Shock dropped Elizabeth's arms from between us. In the few inches separating us, the air vibrated with need.

I erased it. My entire body sighed in relief.

Her face was a breath from mine.

"This has been a long time coming. I've just been too dense to see it for what it is. You *are* the kind of girl I'm looking for, Elizabeth. The only girl I'm looking for."

Tentative fingers fluttered up to brush over my bottom lip. "I'm scared of this."

I smiled beneath them before I brought my hand up to hold hers, pressed her fingers to my mouth in a gentle kiss. "All I'm scared of is losing you."

Elizabeth softened, body and soul.

I could feel it, the way the tension scattered like a gust of wind through a mound of fallen leaves. I took a chance and carefully wound her in my arms.

There was no hesitation from her, just the softness of her hands as they ran up and over my shoulders and anchored at the back of my neck.

I leaned in and swept my nose along the sweetness of her jaw, and I whispered at her ear, "Be with me."

Elizabeth swayed and rocked, and then precious girl let herself go in the security of my arms.

Her face was hidden in the crook of my neck, buried in my need and the absolute devotion I felt for her.

Her mouth pressed to my skin.

It had to be the best thing I'd ever felt.

I danced with her, lifting her from her feet and slowly spinning her around.

We stayed that way for what seemed like forever, the snow flitting down around us while Elizabeth and I said nothing, just allowed our hearts to dance together in an eternal promise.

Because I was never going to let her go.

She pulled her head away to find my face, and I placed her back on her feet. One hand remained firm around her waist, and I brushed aside the hair stuck to the side of her face with the other.

Contentment thrummed in my chest, while my

need for Elizabeth only grew.

Her eyes were all alight, tender, that honeyed-amber swimming with what I felt beating steadily within my heart.

From the moment I saw her, I knew something about her was different. I'd just never imagined it would change my life.

It was Elizabeth who pushed the moment. She lifted to her toes and pressed her lips to mine. Her mouth came so cautious and slow, testing, though I felt nothing there that told me she was still unsure.

The questions between us no longer remained.

Both my hands slid to her hips, and I pulled her as close as I possibly could then wound one hand back up her spine to the base of her neck.

I kissed her slowly.

Savored her unhurriedly.

There was nothing carnal to this kiss. But still, it was enough to reignite the ache she'd left me with for so many months.

Hell, this girl had managed it with one look.

I smiled against her lips, still unable to grasp that she'd brought me this far.

I could feel her grinning, too, before she pulled back. She pressed her lips together as if savoring the remnant of our kiss. "What?"

I shook my head, gripping her tight. "Nothing. I just didn't realize anything could make me this happy."

She hid her face in my chest and mumbled, "Neither did I."

I dropped a kiss to her head and hugged her a little more. She shivered again. Who knew how much time had passed since we'd been standing out in the snow without our jackets.

I stepped back and grabbed two of her fingers because I found I really didn't want to let her go. "You should get inside. It's freezing out here."

She cast a quick glance behind her at her building. The single window to her apartment remained a darkened square against the gray wall.

She turned back to me. "You want to come inside?"

Did I? My body answered with a resounding *Hell, yeah.*

No doubt, the second we crossed her threshold it would be all over. There'd be hands and flesh and need that would no longer be denied.

No longer could anything or anyone stop this attraction that had grown, transformed, and solidified as this bond that could not be broken.

My eyes skimmed over her face. Even though she looked up at me with the same desires that spun a path through my veins and coiled in my muscles, I didn't miss the weariness that lay as purple smudges beneath her eyes.

I shook my head. "No, not tonight."

Disappointment creased her forehead, and I drew her to me and kissed her again. I pushed my mouth near her ear and murmured, "Of course, I *want* to, Elizabeth."

I flattened myself to her so she'd know how much I really did.

"But I'm not going to. Let's do dinner tomorrow, instead. I want that time with you, just knowing it's you and me. Can we do that?"

She sighed and nodded against my chest before she smiled lightly up at me. "Yeah, I'd like that."

I dropped a small kiss to her mouth plus one against her nose. "Do me a favor and go climb underneath a blanket. You're frozen."

She laughed. "Okay."

She stepped back and hooked her index finger with mine. She swayed our hands between us. "I'll miss you."

I'd been missing her for months, and I didn't even know it. "Me, too. I'll see you tomorrow, though, okay?"

Finally, she dropped her hand, turned, and walked away. At the door, she paused to look at me. "It's a date," she told me with a soft smile.

All I could think about was the first day in that café. The smile that lit on my face was to match.

Finally, she pulled the door open and slipped inside.

I wrapped my arms over my chest in an attempt

to shield myself from the cold, my attention trained upstairs. Her light flicked on. Five seconds later, Elizabeth pressed her face to the window. She smiled this wistful smile and placed both hands against the glass.

I stood there with my hands shoved in my pockets, rocking back on my heels as I stared up at her. That spot inside expanded and I loved her a little more.

No one could ever come close to this girl, the way she made me feel, what she made me see. We belonged together.

I lifted a hand in a small wave. Her fingers curled on the window, and her expression filled with that same tenderness she had looked at me with for so long. I hoped she could see the same in mine.

eleven

ELIZABETH

The knock at my door jerked me to my feet. My thoughts raced everywhere, and my nerves only skyrocketed knowing who awaited me on the other side of the door.

I hurried across the room, sidestepping my purse. I'd dropped it in the middle of the floor when I came in last night and rushed to the window to catch another glimpse of Christian before he walked away.

I guessed I'd needed an affirmation. Something to prove what had just transpired between us had been real. And it was, there in his expression, the same thing I felt reflected back at me.

Of course, I'd known I was in love with him before, though the realization had gutted me. Rather than joy, I'd felt only pain, my feelings for him nothing more than a millstone around my neck.

But last night had changed everything and peering down at him had revealed something greater to me. Joy had firmly taken root in my heart as a future unfolded before my eyes, snapped into place like the jagged pieces of a puzzle, ones that didn't seem to fit but always belonged together.

We'd been raised so differently. Maybe it was those differences that made us so perfect for each other.

I opened the door to Christian standing there with his hands shoved deep in his coat pockets.

That mass of hair on his head was mussed, framing his pretty face. A clean shave had erased any trace of the shadow that usually had set by this time of day.

It accentuated every sharp line and contour of his jaw. The curve of a gentle smile lifted one side of his mouth.

"Hey," he said, his head tilting to the side. He drew his shoulders up as his face bled into a timid grin.

"Hey." I could feel the flush make its way up

my neck to tint my cheeks.

Being around Christian had never been easy. It'd always been a feat of wills, brute strength and iron-clad resolve. I'd become almost accustomed to it until I stood before him now.

With all of our reservations out of way, I felt like a different girl.

Blue eyes gleamed as they traveled along my face and kissed along the length of my body.

Thick laughter jutted from his throat as he took me in.

I bit back a smile as another rush of heat flared on my face.

This morning when I'd talked to him on the phone, he asked me to wear the same thing I'd worn to the party last Friday. I knew under his coat he'd be wearing the same tight black T-shirt, and that his dark jeans would be a taunting me from where they hung low on his hips

He wanted a redo.

I wanted one, too.

"Come here," he said under his breath, one hand reaching out to beckon me forward.

I didn't hesitate to nestle into his chest.

He wrapped both arms around me, rocked me as he hugged me close. Gentle lips pressed to the top of my head.

"You look amazing." I felt his laughter rather than heard it. "Why didn't I just tell you before?"

His voice dropped as he burrowed his mouth farther into my hair. "Why couldn't I just tell you I wanted to make love to you? Touch you and hold you because you were the one who was meant for me?"

Tingles shot down my spine with his words, and I nuzzled my nose deeper into his chest.

"Why didn't I tell you I was confused and scared by everything you made me feel instead of running away from you?" he added.

Shaking my head, I looked at him. "I don't regret it at all, Christian. I'm mean, don't get me wrong . . . last week hurt . . . and I hate having spent those days without you, but I have to believe it finally forced us to admit things we were too scared to see. If it hadn't have happened, I'd probably be sitting on your couch instead of standing here like this with you."

I clung to him and whispered, "And this is really where I want to be."

Christian's hands came up to cup my jaw, gently prodding. I lifted my eyes to his. Emotion softened every hard angle of his face, and that place reserved for him fluttered inside. He dipped his head and pressed a sweet kiss to the edge of my mouth.

"This is the only place I want to be, Elizabeth . . . with you."

My forehead fell back to his chest to hide the

heat that rushed to my cheeks. I breathed him in, loved the way he smelled, loved everything about him.

There was no more holding back, no more questioning what we were or where we were going.

"Are you ready to get out of here?" he asked.

"Yeah." I stepped back.

"Be sure to grab a warm coat and a scarf. It's freezing out there."

I nodded and turned back into my studio to gather my things.

Christian followed right behind and stood in the middle of my apartment.

Just watching me.

I kept glancing up at him, and each time it was the same. I'd catch him with the same expression on his face, the one that fluttered my pulse and sent a tumult of butterflies tipping through my stomach.

Hands shaking, I struggled to pull my heavy coat over my sweatshirt.

He stepped to me, his voice all breathy and matching everything I felt inside. "Here . . . let me help you with that."

He slipped the coat over my shoulders and tugged at the collar to straighten it. He grinned when it caused me to stumble forward into him. Leaning in close, he reached behind me to free the hair trapped in the confines of my coat and ran his long fingers through the length with a satisfied smile coming over his face.

"Do you have any idea how many times I've imagined my hands in your hair." He lifted a handful and slowly let each piece fall away, the strands tickling at my neck as his sweet breath trickled over my face.

I couldn't help but laugh as I buttoned my coat, my brow cinching with a playful scowl. "Oh, I distinctly remember them being there before. Have you forgotten so easily?" I was surprised by the tease that found its way from my mouth.

But I didn't want that night to be remembered as an obstacle, when in reality, it'd been our launching pad.

A throaty chuckle seeped into the room, and Christian shook his head as he placed his hands on my hips. "No, Elizabeth, I haven't forgotten. That night has been ingrained in my mind as one of the best and worst nights of my life . . . the night I first kissed you and was foolish enough to lose you in the same heartbeat."

All pretenses fell from his face, and his hands tightened their hold. "I promise you—that will never happen again."

I believed it—I wouldn't accept him any other way.

Something like distress darkened his eyes. "I mean it, Elizabeth. This is it for me."

My fingers came up to coax his worry lines away from his brow. "I know, Christian." My palm slid down his cheek to rest on the steady tick of his pulse in his neck. I wet my lips and made my own promise. "*I trust you.*"

Relief flooded him, loosening his tense muscles and chasing the storm from his eyes, my words the cure for whatever vestiges of doubt that still remained.

Taking one step back, he grabbed my hand and brought the back to his lips. The heavy moment was gone. In its place, I sensed his thrill. It spilled over onto me.

"Come on." He hauled me toward the door. "I want to take you out. You denied me this before, you know."

A smirk arched his brow, this playful ease coming over us, one we'd shared so many times, but with our barriers still set firmly in place.

This was liberating.

I squeezed his hand and worked to keep up as I followed him out the door. "Where are we going?"

"You'll see." He tossed a grin back at me, and I pulled the door shut behind us.

He led me out and down the hall, didn't let go as he dragged me into the stairwell. As always, it was dim, the walls seemingly compressed, the air instantly tight. Just being in its confines, alone with him, escalated my heart rate.

I gasped when Christian abruptly turned and pushed me up against the wall. His mouth crashed into mine as he covered me with his body.

This kiss was hot, demanding, filled with every ounce of the desire we'd kept restrained for far too long.

My fingers dug into his neck as his fingers dug into my backside.

And I loved it.

Every second.

God, I loved him.

When he pulled away, much too soon, he was panting, his blue eyes wild and his mouth dancing with a smug, satisfied smile. "Do you have any idea how many times I wanted to do that? This fucking stairwell has been the bane of my existence for the last four months."

A strained laugh fluttered from my mouth, doing nothing to disguise the intense need that tightened my voice. "You felt that, too, huh?"

He laughed and shook his head, his posture softening as he drew me closer and completely wrapped me up in his secure arms. "You don't even understand, Elizabeth. You've pretty much made me think I was losing my mind since the moment I met you."

My head dropped to his chest, my fingers playing along the buttons of his coat as I averted my gaze. I loved hearing him voice it, to touch me and tell me he had felt the same way I did. "I'm pretty sure I do."

I risked peeking up at him. God, he was beautiful. Every inch, angle, and curve.

"How did we manage to stay away from each other for this long?"

My hands fisted in his jacket. "Honestly, I have no clue."

Grabbing my hand again, he guided me down the rest of the steps and out into the cold. The sun had set a couple hours earlier and the city had come alive. Cars and taxis filled the streets, the lights glowing overhead in the frosty air.

I shivered, and Christian wrapped an arm around my waist. I cuddled into the warmth of his side. He planted a kiss on my temple.

I exhaled and snuggled closer.

This was nothing short of perfection.

We walked down to the intersection where it was easier to find a cab. I hopped in the first we could find, Christian laughing as he climbed in behind me. He pulled me right to his side, sloppily kissing me under my jaw.

Everything soared, a sensation of weightlessness washing me in joy.

"Where to?" the cabbie asked.

Wide eyed and teasing, I jerked my head to face him. "Yeah, where to?"

Christian rambled off the address as he draped

his arm over my shoulder.

Downtown.

The ride was short, and I was laughing outright by the time Christian was pulling me from the cab and running us in the direction of The Rink at Rockefeller Center.

"We're going ice skating? Are you serious?" I yelled at the back of his gorgeous head as he twisted us through the crowd, his hand firm on mine, never letting go.

He looked back at me, so carefree.

My best friend.

His hands were in my hair, pressed to the sides of my head when he whirled around to kiss me in the middle of the roving crowd. "Where else would I take my girl except where she wants to go?"

He paid for our tickets and skates, both of us fumbling, cracking up as we put on our skates and tentatively ventured out onto the ice.

His hands were never far, his mouth at my neck, at my ear, and at my mouth. Our words were flirty, easy, exactly what I wanted us to be.

My best friend.

He kissed me against the railing, when I fell and he helped me up, when we returned our skates and wandered hand-in-hand back out into the city.

He stopped in front of a large window at a little pizza place. Candles glowed from each round table crammed into the small space. "How's this?"

"Looks good."

We were seated toward the back. It was quaint inside, nothing fancy, just the two of us and a natural flow of conversation. Effortless.

We ordered a pizza to share, neither of us hesitating to dig in as soon as it was served.

Under the table, his hand rested on my knee, his thumb a constant caress.

He took a bite of pizza and glanced up at me with affection swimming in his eyes.

Never had I imagined ending up with someone like him. What I had pictured, I wasn't quite sure.

Safe, I supposed.

Simple and plain.

Someone who worked hard and loved just because he should. Someone who wanted a family and an easy life. Someone who I'd meet years in the future.

But Christian was none of those things. He was complicated, both selfish and kind, thoughtful and mindless, generous with a tendency toward greed.

And he was anything but plain. This beautiful man stole my breath with a simple look and had me shaking with the mere brush of his hand.

Once, Christian had been a mistake I couldn't afford. Now, he'd become someone I didn't want to live without. My pulse stuttered as I looked at him.

He looked so much like the type of guy I'd

sworn never to give myself to. My heart recognized the risk. He could so easily crush me, but Christian had become my welcomed complication.

Black hair brushed over his forehead as he cocked his head to the side in a silent question, obviously wondering where my thoughts had wandered.

"It's nothing," I mumbled low, dragging a napkin over my mouth to cover the emotion building there.

Crinkles lighted at the corners of his eyes as he mildly frowned, and he only squeezed my knee.

Christian chatted on as if we'd been together for years. Plans for our future were made without thought, where he would take me and the different things he wanted us to experience together. How different school would be now that we didn't have to pretend, how our lives seemed fated as they had finally aligned.

The waitress brought our check and Christian set a credit card on the tray. After he paid, he silently rose and extended his hand.

My chair squeaked on the tile floor as I pushed back from the table and accepted Christian's waiting hand. He said nothing as he helped me back into my coat and wrapped my scarf around my neck, the gesture quietly intimate.

All traces of the light mood from earlier had evaporated, a charge igniting the air.

"Ready?"

Swallowing, I intertwined my fingers with his. "Yes."

In silence, we snaked between the tiny tables filling the dark restaurant. Christian held the door open for me, and I stepped out.

Cold had increased its hold on the city.

A chill slid down my spine, and I hugged my arms across my chest.

From behind, Christian cocooned himself around me. Covering my hands with his, he drew me tight against him and hooked his jaw over my shoulder.

His breath washed over me, so thick and warm—sweet and kind—his nose nuzzling behind my ear, his lips sending shivers down the sensitive skin.

Then he pressed his cheek against mine.

"I love you, Elizabeth."

It was said so easily, bled so naturally. I harbored no questions of its truth.

"I love you, Christian, so much." The words filtered out ahead of us and mingled with the night air.

Christian had stolen my heart and held it in his hand.

Without letting go, he edged us forward, said nothing as he lifted his hand to hail a cab. He opened the door and gently eased me down into the back seat. Soundlessly, he slipped in and wrapped me back in his arms.

He murmured my address into the darkened cab.

The driver pulled into traffic.

Turned to the side, I rested my cheek over the beat of his heart. One of his arms held me close, his fingers playing in my hair, his other hand gripping mine on his lap.

I could feel it, the strained ripples of need coursing between us, this new uncertainty, another question.

Tension ricocheted between us. His hand tightened in mine, and he turned to whisper in my ear. "Come home with me, Elizabeth. I don't want to take you home."

"I never said I wanted you to."

The gust of air he released from his nose rustled through my hair at the top of my head. The sound reflected the moment, relief and tension and building anticipation.

Christian shifted me so he could lean forward.

"Excuse me. We've had a change of plans." Christian gave him his address. The driver nodded and turned down the next street in the direction of Christian's apartment.

We settled back into silence.

Waiting.

Wanting.

The short ride felt too long. Christian paid the fare and climbed from the backseat, never once losing the hold he had on me.

He glanced back over his shoulder as he lightly tugged at my hand.

Slowly, he led us inside his building and up the three long flights of stairs.

Expectation swelled between us, echoed in our footsteps and in the heavy breaths we forced in and out of our lungs.

I clung to him, my hand tight in his, the other wrapped around his wrist as he walked a step ahead of me.

I was nervous.

Excited.

Terrified.

Not of *this*, but of what I didn't know, of all my inadequacies and deficiencies.

He stopped at his door and fumbled through his pockets to withdraw his keys. Metal scraped as the key was inserted in the keyhole, the sound piercing in the hush of the hall.

Christian pushed the door open wide, pulled me in behind him, and spun to close it in the same movement he edged me up against it.

Cold fingertips brushed over my cheeks and down my jaw. He began to slowly unwind the scarf from my neck.

Christian's eyes were all ablaze, smoldering as he

stared me down.

Cherishing.

He slipped the scarf from my neck and dropped it to the floor. He palmed the heated flesh there, sent chills flying through my system.

"You're shaking," he said.

My tongue darted out to wet my lips, and I looked up at him and answered him with all the honesty I had. "I'm a little nervous."

Okay.

Maybe not completely honest.

I was really nervous, so out of my element. My body quaked uncontrollably, these long rolls of trembles that I couldn't stop no matter how hard I tried. They vibrated between us. Palpable. Clear.

Sex had left a rancid taste in my mouth. A bitter mark on my soul.

But I wanted this. I had for so long. I wanted to explore what Christian had created in me.

The arc of his mouth was tender. "Elizabeth, whatever happens tonight is totally up to you. I'm not going to lie. I've been dying to make love to you since the first time I met you, and whenever you let me, I will cherish it. But I don't want it until you're ready."

"It's not that." My gaze dropped for a beat. "I . . . I just don't want to disappoint you."

"God, Elizabeth." He blinked hard, and his hold intensified on either side of my neck. Raging blue eyes opened to me. "You couldn't. It's not even possible. Is that really what you're worried about?"

Chewing on the inside of my lip, I nodded.

This anxious sound seeped from the back of his throat, and he dropped his arms. "I've never been so nervous in my life."

"What? Why?" The words tripped from my mouth as one.

"Because it's you, and I don't want to mess this up. When I touch you"—he reached up to trace a straight line from my chin to the hollow at the base of my neck—"I don't want to leave behind any question of how much I love you."

His low laugh was almost pained. "And what I want most is to wipe the memory of anyone else touching you from your mind."

Again, our distinct differences made us the same.

"All I want is you, Christian." With my gaze pinned on him, I fumbled to let the first button of his coat free. "For us to forget everything and everyone else, because none of that matters anymore."

I was still shaking as I worked through the rest of his buttons. Christian just stood there, watching me. When I finally released them, I pressed my palms to his chest and ran them up to push his coat off his shoulders.

Christian's muscles twitched, jerking at the

contact.

Shrugging the rest of the way out of his coat, Christian tossed it to his couch, turned and slowly unbuttoned mine. He threw it on top of his.

Then he stepped back and took me in. His gaze slid softly from my face, his eyes flicking to the exposed skin at my shoulder, to my breasts, caressed down my jeans, and back up again.

He took my hand. "Come here."

His room was down the short hall.

It was dark inside, and I could only make out the subtle silhouette of his bed in the backdrop of night. He pulled me behind him as he went to his desk along the opposite wall. He flicked on the small lamp resting at the far corner of the desk, clicking through to the lowest setting.

It cast the room in a faint glow, illuminated his beautiful face with subdued light.

I reached out to trace his face, my fingertips trailing over the sharp angles and the bold lines. I smoothed my touch against his strong brow and played along his soft lips.

Christian just barely kissed them, his lips parting as I freely explored.

I felt the smile on my mouth. "You're so beautiful," I whispered.

Christian laughed quietly, as if what I'd spoken was absurd. "Look at you, Elizabeth." His fingers tickled along my collarbone. "You are perfect."

His mouth caressed along mine as one of his hands twisted in the mass of my hair. The other burned into the small of my back.

I snaked my hands under his shirt. My touch was fevered as I splayed my hands and ran them up his stomach, to his shoulders, and tore his shirt over his head.

What hid under Christian's shirt was glorious.

Lean, taut muscles jumped beneath my hands. Christian sucked in a desperate breath. "One touch, and you're killing me already, Elizabeth."

A smile twitched on his flirty mouth, but his expression spoke of so much more than that. This was a need that had captured us, a love that had left us completely undone.

His mouth went to my shoulder. "Do you remember that night?" He tugged my collar farther off my shoulder and pressed his teeth into my skin.

My breath caught.

It wasn't enough to hurt, just enough to weaken my knees.

I clung to his arms. I knew he wouldn't let me fall.

"This right here is what finally threw me over the edge." He kissed along my flesh, drawing in a shaky breath as his hands made their way under my sweatshirt. Heated palms grazed my sides.

Slowly he dragged my shirt over my head, his gaze drifting down over the black lace of my strapless bra. With a single finger, he traced over the lace ridges of the cup. His face was painfully close when he reached around with both hands to unclasp its hold.

It fell away, and goosebumps flashed across my flesh.

I swallowed the thick knot that formed in my throat when Christian stepped back and brazenly contemplated me in nothing but my jeans, his eyes roaming, memorizing.

And it wasn't awkward or any of the things I worried it might be.

Christian reached out and dragged his knuckles over the bud of my breast. "You are perfect," he said again.

One hand slipped to the back of my neck and the other grasped my side, his mouth urgent on mine as our bare chests met.

I caught fire.

"Christian," I begged through a whimper.

"I know, baby, I know," he mumbled between kisses, nudging me back toward his bed. He eased me down onto it, and I grasped at him when he didn't follow.

He caught my hands, climbed to his knees on the bed as he pinned them over my head, left them there as he traveled down my body and kissed me on my belly as he slowly unbuttoned my jeans.

I was gasping for air.

He got back to his feet, pulled them from my legs, and dropped them to the floor.

He stood at the end of his bed where he'd left me in only my panties, my knees twisted to one side and my arms draped over my head.

I felt exposed.

Vulnerable.

For the first time in my life, I wanted to be.

He was so beautiful as he stood there soaking up every inch of my body. My eyes wandered and did the same, watching as he slowly released each button on his jeans.

He pushed them down, stepped out, and kicked them aside.

Heat flooded my face as I took in Christian in nothing but a pair of tight boxer briefs. My heart beat fast, spurred on by this insane desire to touch him and for him to touch me.

Kneeling on the edge of his bed, he gently spread my knees apart with both hands. He dipped his head, dropped a kiss to my inner thigh, and crawled the rest of the way up my body to settle between my legs.

I gripped his shoulders, and Christian brushed his fingers along my cheek, smiled down at me before he kissed me long and slow. He rained those kisses along my jaw, pressed them to my chest, captured my breast in his mouth.

I was adrift, my fingers in his hair as Christian's

skimmed up and down my sides. My body vibrated, resonating with emotion.

He rose to his hands and abruptly his shoulders dropped as he dove down to press his mouth to my hipbone.

I sucked in a sharp breath as my hips jerked from the bed.

He rocked back up on his hands, his eyes chaotic as he stared at me. He didn't look away as he wrapped his hands around my waist, his fingers sliding down to gather the edges of my panties. He wound his fingers through, palmed my backside.

I was half exposed.

A suppressed moan broke from his mouth. "You have the sweetest ass, Elizabeth." He squeezed once before he shimmied my panties down, for one second shifting to my side to pull them off.

I was squirming, this unknown need Christian had created in me knotting my every muscle.

Kneeling between my legs, Christian stared at me as he grazed the back of his hand up my inner thigh. "I'm going to touch you, okay?" His voice was hoarse, his attention flicking down between my legs then back up to me.

Somewhere inside, I searched for embarrassment, to find a reason to be ashamed.

But it was nowhere to be found.

This wasn't like the few second fumbles I'd had

with Ryan. This wouldn't leave me feeling dirty and used, and Christian would never send me away disappointed.

"Please."

Christian watched over me as I looked up at him. His fingers found me. My mouth went dry.

In seconds, I was breathless, unable to fathom how free I felt, this need to experience with Christian everything I'd never experienced before.

My back arched as pleasure built.

And I was saying his name, begging, pleading, because he was driving something in me no one had ever managed to reach before.

It twisted tighter.

Wound higher.

Then it broke.

Pleasure streaked through my body, and I cried out as I dug my heels into his bed.

Christian braced himself with one hand, dipping down to kiss my stomach as he led me through my release.

My entire being slumped to the bed, overflowing with satisfaction that oozed and bled, shone as sweat across my body and contented every crevice in my heart.

"Oh my God," I breathed.

A low rumble echoed from Christian's chest as he crawled back over me and pressed his mouth against mine.

"You are amazing," he mumbled between kisses.

"Pretty sure that was all you. And yeah, amazing." I kissed him hard.

I felt him smiling against my mouth, his fingers winding in my hair. "Yeah?"

"Um, yeah. Definitely yeah."

He pushed up on his hands. A look of adoration crossed over his face, this softness that radiated from his spirit while every inch of his body remained hard, twitching as he held himself in restraint.

I stared up at him as he caged me, my hands shaking as I reached between us to push his underwear from his hips.

"Elizabeth . . . baby . . ." His voice came in a harsh whisper as he tucked his chin to look between us where I struggled to get them down past his thighs.

He moaned, twisting out of them while he continued to hover over me, and kicked them off his feet.

He turned his face back to me. He clenched his jaw when I wrapped one hand around him and the other around the back of his neck.

A shudder traveled from his pelvis, over the ridges of his perfect stomach and up his chest, emitted as a stuttered breath from his lips that spread across my face.

"Elizabeth," he rasped, blue eyes boring into mine as his tongue darted out to wet his lips.

Lust flared in his eyes, and he clutched the sheets on either side of me. He rocked into my hand, muscles rippling along his back, bunching over his shoulders.

Fragmented tremors rolled through my body as I surrendered to this abandon. I'd never understood what it felt like to both desire and feel desired. I sucked in a strained breath as I explored him, my eyes never leaving his face, feasting on the pleasure I brought him.

He reached down and covered my hand with his. "Elizabeth, baby . . . I think you need to stop. That feels way too good and this is not how I imagined ending this night."

Christian kept a hand on my hip as he rushed to sit up, tore open his side drawer, and rummaged around inside. He pulled out a little foil packet and ripped it between his teeth.

My legs shook as he knelt on his knees between my thighs. Air heaved in and out of my lungs as unbridled need spun with a loose thread of apprehension.

It coiled as a hunger deep in my stomach, throbbed between my legs.

Christian quickly covered himself, his hands coming down to run up the underside of my thighs as he tugged me closer to him. My legs dropped open to make him room.

Fire singed the fibers of my skin as Christian slid his palms up my body and down my arms to lace his fingers with mine, then brought them between on chests. His elbows hit the bed, bracketing my body, his weight propped by the easy bend of his knees. Our hands were tied between us, our chests rising and falling in spastic quakes.

Christian nudged the side of my face with his nose. I felt him breathe me in, felt an impossible connection with this man who hovered above me. His mouth grazed the side of my face, his voice soft in my ear. "I love you so much, Elizabeth."

His nose traveled my cheek until he brought us face to face. His expression was severe, twisted lines of devotion and lust.

So beautiful.

He swallowed deeply and shifted. I felt him at my center. He barely marked me, the slightest penetration as he searched for air and his hands tightened on mine. But he didn't look away. Searching. Longing. Loving.

"I love you," I whispered, the words a promise, an encouragement that I wanted this as much as he did.

There was no turning back, nothing I could do to win back my heart.

Christian swept a gentle kiss across my lips before he pulled back an inch to look down on me.

He tightened his hold as he gathered me closer.

Then he slowly filled me.

His elbows dug farther into the bed and his mouth dropped open with a ragged grunt.

An overdose of sensations hastened through my nerves as Christian took all of me. He seared into my body as he stretched me, the burn the most exquisite kind of pain. It was a branding. A seal. And I'd never be the same.

Now Christian held me whole. This was a bond we could not break.

For a few seconds, we both lay still and listened to the short gasps heaving from our lungs and the blood pounding through our veins. Nose to nose, we stared.

Christian unwound our hands, shifted to bring one to my face. Tender fingers brushed back the hair clinging to my damp forehead.

And he smiled. This stomach-flipping, heart-lurching, earth-shattering smile. But it no longer was a smile of manipulation, not one to bend me to his way. This one was genuine, filled with love and adoration and everything I wanted us to be.

This smile was only for me.

"Are you okay?" he murmured. He splayed his hand wide, his fingers supporting the back of my head while his thumb caressed over my cheek.

I wet my lips, taking in the man above me, the only one I would ever love. My fingertips fluttered over his lips, and I whispered, "Perfect."

I tilted my chin and lifted my mouth to his. The kiss started slow, soft and tender, flicks of tongue and grazes of teeth, as tender and slow as the movements of his body as he cautiously began to move within me.

Pressed together, he kissed me deeper, our mouths filled with longing as I opened to him, body and soul. I ran my hands over his shoulders and down his back. The muscles were rigid and strained as they bowed and twisted as he worked over me.

Tentatively I moved, lifting my hips to meet him.

Christian slipped one hand down my side, his fingertips digging into the ridges between my ribs. A smooth palm cupped my bottom before he flattened it over my hip and ran it down to my knee. He tucked me closer and hooked my leg over his hip.

Pulling back, he filled me, deliberate and strong.

I gasped and clung to his shoulders as I began to match him move for move.

"Oh, God, Elizabeth." His fingers dug deep into my thigh. Incoherent mutterings of pleasure slipped from his mouth to mine, and I devoured them while he devoured me.

That feeling built again.

Everything was frantic, the love that solidified

this bond between us, the sounds that filled his room, mumbled words of devotion, every desperate touch.

I knew he was getting close. His movements were quick, jerky, his breaths clipped and labored. "Elizabeth . . . uh . . . you feel so good. So . . . good."

This time he was begging and I was clinging because I needed more.

His hand slipped between us because Christian knew.

I curved my arm around his head, and he buried his face in the crook of my neck.

And I was lost.

Lost to him.

Pleasure rushed, surged and crashed, saturated every inch of my body.

Christian jerked and cried out in my neck, held himself rigid before all the strength left him and he collapsed on me.

We lay like that for countless minutes, our worlds shaken.

Christian rolled to his side, taking me with him. He placed his palm on my cheek, caressed this thumb over the edge of my lips. He gazed at me as if I were the center of his world.

There was nothing I could have done to stop this when I realized he'd become mine. "I'm going to love you forever, Elizabeth Ayers."

I looked up at the man who now held everything, my trust, my future, the nature of my heart. Reaching up, I ran my fingers through the thickness of his black hair.

"Don't ever leave me, Christian."

Christian frowned, his blue eyes sincere as he leaned forward to whisper at my forehead. "I couldn't."

twelve

CHRISTIAN

"Christian, let go." She struggled to untangle herself from my arms that were wrapped tight around her waist. The only thing it did was cause me to tighten my hold.

She giggled and pushed against my chest.

My words came muffled into the crook of her neck where I pressed my mouth against her skin. "No, stay."

I didn't want her to be anywhere else.

"I wish I could, but I have to get to class." She pulled back, and I was unable to stop my smile as I looked into the warmth of those honeyed eyes.

God, I loved her so much. That hadn't lessened in the four years we'd been together. It'd only grown.

I pretended to pout but released my hold, allowing her to roll away from me.

A faint smile tugged at my mouth as I turned to lie on my stomach.

There was nothing else I could do but watch her dress in the late evening light filtering in through the blinds of my bedroom window.

Elizabeth leaned down to pull her jeans onto her long, toned legs.

Locks of dark-blonde hair cascaded in messy waves over her shoulder, obstructing her small, heart-shaped face.

Though every line, dimple, and curve had been burned into my mind.

Everything about her made me think of honey.

The honey tinge of her eyes, the sun kiss of her skin, the sweetness of her mouth.

I should have known the moment I met her that she was perfect for me. I should have known it with the way she'd stolen my breath the second I'd walked through the doors of that small café and found the girl sitting there waiting for me—my study partner that had become my everything.

She was not only beautiful but one of the most intelligent, compassionate people I'd ever met.

Over the last four years, I'd gotten to know her in the best of ways.

In every way.

Our lives had meshed.

Become one.

Neither of us wanted it any other way.

We were so different, yet so much alike.

Like me, she had continued to work her way toward law school next year. But while I'd become a real estate attorney so I could one day partner in my father's law firm, Elizabeth would be going into family law, focusing on children's rights.

She wasn't in it for the money.

She thought it was the best way for her to become an advocate for those who could not protect themselves.

She still left me in awe every day.

"Are you sure you have to go?"

She grinned over at me. "Aren't you the one who's always saying we have to stay focused on our studies?"

I smirked at her. "I changed my mind."

Light laughter filtered from her mouth. "I don't think so, Christian. Not today. Besides, I have work first thing in the morning. Matthew will kill me if I end up crawling in that bed with you and don't show up for my shift tomorrow."

"Forget Matthew," I teased.

Maybe I should have been jealous of Matthew.

He'd become one of Elizabeth's best friends, and they studied together often after getting to know each other at work when Elizabeth had started at a small restaurant a couple of years ago.

But I wasn't.

With the way she looked at me, there was no questioning her devotion to me.

She was good.

True.

I guessed I'd known it that first day all those years ago when I'd listened to the passion that had come from Elizabeth's mouth.

Honestly, it'd made me question myself—what I believed in and what I lived for.

Over time, that answer had become clear.

Elizabeth.

She made me a better person.

The best part was our goals perfectly aligned.

Our lives planned out.

She was serious about school and committed to her future, but she still took time to enjoy every day of her life, something I'd had a hard time balancing at first.

My father had always pushed me to do the best, to *be* the best.

Before I'd met her, I'd become arrogant.

Conceited.

Completely wrapped up in myself.

Elizabeth had challenged my self-serving

attitude from the very start.

ELIZABETH

I laughed at the boy who grinned at me from his bed.

I'd never been one for frivolous things—a fling with a beautiful, black-haired, blue-eyed boy included. I'd thought that was the only thing he'd be.

A fling.

That he'd break my heart.

Now I just shook my head at what he'd suggested, no longer surprised by his demand.

By the fact that he always wanted me to stay.

Still, I fought the well of unease that built up inside of me. Nerves rattling through, wondering how in the world I was going to tell him.

Terrified of the way he might react and excited at the same time.

"I'm not forgetting Matthew. That would be rude. Besides, I need the money, and if I stay here with you, you know what's going to happen."

"That's exactly what I was hoping for."

Another one of those grins.

If I stayed any longer, he would definitely have his way.

I shoved my feet into my shoes. "I need to go

home."

"Then move in with me."

Another shot of laughter rippled out, but this one with pure disbelief.

"I think you already know the answer to that."

"I want a different one."

Christian had asked me so many times to move in with him.

I couldn't help but find the idea of waking up next to him each morning incredibly inviting.

But that didn't matter.

I'd always quietly refused, committed to the picture I had painted in my mind from childhood.

It was one of a new house with a new husband, a place where I would become mother and he would become father, though now I found that picture skewed.

Again, I glanced over my shoulder at Christian as I prepared to leave.

A wave of guilt washed over me for keeping it from him for so long.

I'd known for a week.

Every day, I intended to tell him, but each time I opened my mouth, the words just wouldn't come.

Even with the progress I'd seen him make, growing from the self-centered teenager I'd met our first year here at Columbia to the kind-hearted man I knew now, Christian still had his life mapped out.

A plan he intended to follow.

I wasn't exactly sure of how he was going to handle this news.

I wasn't concerned about our relationship. I felt confident in our commitment to one another.

We were solid.

What I was worried about was how much stress this would place on him. This wasn't exactly what I'd expected of my last year of under-grad before law school, either.

I was just better at accepting what life threw my way.

But we'd figure it out.

I knew we would.

Before I spiraled into worry, I grabbed my backpack, slung it over my shoulder, and leaned down, planting a quick kiss on Christian's lips.

"Bye. I'll see you tomorrow."

He returned the kiss, lingering a little longer than I had, stirring those feelings inside of me.

Making me want to say *forget* it like he'd suggested and crawl right back in bed with him.

"I'll miss you," he murmured.

"Miss you, too."

Forcing myself to turn around, I flew out the door of Christian's third-floor apartment.

With each step, my feet grew heavier as my mind wandered.

Wondering about the best way to tell him.

How I was going to tell him.

Something in my stomach souring when I thought of it being a betrayal that I hadn't let him in.

This was just as important to him as it was to me.

By the time I reached the last set of stairs leading to the ground floor, I realized I just needed to get it out.

Tell him before I let it fester. Before I made it dirty. Before it became a sin.

I turned and raced back up the stairs.

I had a key, but for some reason, I felt the need to knock as another rush of nerves wound around my chest.

Sucking in a deep breath, I rapped loudly on his door.

CHRISTIAN

A loud knock thundered on the main door. I jerked, not expecting anyone, quick to climb out of bed and pull on my jeans from the floor. I ran a hand through the thick mass of my black hair and ambled out of my room and toward the door.

Peering through the peephole, I caught sight of Elizabeth standing on the other side.

Confusion hit me. Why in the world was she

standing outside my door, asking permission to enter?

Like she didn't belong there.

Frowning, I swung open the door. "Elizabeth, what are you doing?"

"I need to talk to you." The distinct anxiety laced through the words sent a jolt of fear tumbling through me.

Quickly, I pulled her inside and shut the door, spinning around to face her.

"What's wrong?" Obviously, there was something wrong, or she wouldn't have been standing in my apartment, staring at her feet with rigid arms held over her chest.

"I'm pregnant."

It was a whisper toward the floor.

A breath.

I strained to hear her. To decipher them. To make sense of what she was saying.

Because there was no way she'd said what I thought she did.

Dread sank to the bottom of me when she finally brought her gaze to me.

Her honey-eyes watery and afraid.

My hands began to shake, and I ran them nervously through my hair again as I allowed myself to really hear her.

To process the implication of what she was saying.

A baby?

That would ruin everything—everything I'd worked for.

Everything she'd worked for.

Every plan we'd ever made.

My chest tightened, and for the first time in my life, I was sure I was going to have a panic attack.

There was a part of me that wanted to demand to know how she could have been so careless.

That was right before the rational side of me knew it had been just as much my fault as hers.

It wasn't like she'd gotten herself into this alone.

It was that same rational side that saw her shaking, and I was struck with the need to comfort her. To tell her it would be okay.

It was the same side that told me not to panic.

We had options.

It didn't have to be that big of a deal.

"Hey," I murmured softly, taking a step forward to wrap her in my arms.

I ran my fingers through her long hair to soothe her. She pressed her face into my chest and released an audible sigh of relief.

"It's okay," I whispered calmly into the side of her head. "It's okay. We'll get it taken care of."

Elizabeth jerked back as if she'd been slapped.

Those eyes searched my face.

"Christian, you don't really expect me to do that, do you?" she asked, incredulous.

As much as I loved her, there were times when she just couldn't see straight through her idealistic mind.

Of course, they'd talked about her beliefs before.

I knew her viewpoint.

But that was before we had been thrown into the situation. It changed things.

It was the only way.

"Elizabeth . . . you have to."

"No."

How could she be so irrational? How could she make this decision for both of us?

How could she stand there and ruin everything?

Anger suddenly slammed me from all sides, and I stepped back and released the words I had no idea how deeply I'd regret.

"Me or the baby. It shouldn't be that hard of a choice."

the end

Continue on with Christian and Elizabeth's story in

TAKE THIS *Regret*

I invite you to sign up for mobile updates to receive short, but sweet updates on all my latest releases.
Text "aljackson" to 33222
(US Only)
or
Sign up for my newsletter
http://smarturl.it./NewsFromALJackson

Watch for my upcoming series, *Confessions of the Heart*, coming Fall 2018!

Want to know when it's live?
Sign up here: http://smarturl.it/liveonamzn

More From A.L. Jackson

ABOUT THE AUTHOR

A.L. Jackson is the New York Times & USA Today Bestselling author of contemporary romance. She writes emotional, sexy, heart-filled stories about boys who usually like to be a little bit bad.

Her bestselling series include THE REGRET SERIES, CLOSER TO YOU, BLEEDING STARS, as well as the newest FIGHT FOR ME novels.

Watch for her new series, CONFESSIONS OF THE HEART, coming Fall 2018

If she's not writing, you can find her hanging out by the pool with her family, sipping cocktails with her friends, or of course with her nose buried in a book.

Be sure not to miss new releases and sales from A.L. Jackson - Sign up to receive her newsletter http://smarturl.it/NewsFromALJackson or text "aljackson" to 33222 to receive short but sweet updates on all the important news.

Connect with A.L. Jackson online:

Page **http://smarturl.it/ALJacksonPage**
Newsletter **http://smarturl.it/NewsFromALJackson**
Angels **http://smarturl.it/AmysAngelsRock**
Amazon **http://smarturl.it/ALJacksonAmzn**
Book Bub **http://smarturl.it/ALJacksonBookbub**
Text "aljackson" to 33222 to receive short but sweet updates on all the important news.

Made in the USA
Middletown, DE
13 December 2022

18450088R00154